"Why did you d[...] those months a[...] wrong?"

She swept a hand over his shoulder. "You didn't do anything wrong."

"Then why'd you walk away from me?"

"My job is dangerous. Every day I leave for work not knowing if I'll make it back home."

Brandon pushed a lock of hair behind her ear. "I've got news for you, Yara. No one knows if they'll make it until the end of the day."

Her eyes focused on his face. "You know what I mean. I never want to put you or anyone through the agony of having to pick up the pieces and go on if something happens to me on the job."

He held her tighter. "What about the agony of never knowing what we could have been because we never tried?"

UNDER THE COVER OF DARKNESS

K.D. RICHARDS

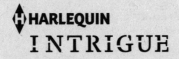

HARLEQUIN
INTRIGUE

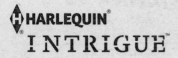

Recycling programs for this product may not exist in your area.

ISBN-13: 978-1-335-59136-4

Under the Cover of Darkness

Harlequin Enterprises ULC
22 Adelaide St. West, 41st Floor
Toronto, Ontario M5H 4E3, Canada
www.Harlequin.com

Printed in U.S.A.

K.D. Richards is a native of the Washington, DC, area, who now lives outside Toronto with her husband and two sons. You can find her at kdrichardsbooks.com.

Books by K.D. Richards

Harlequin Intrigue

West Investigations

Visit the Author Profile page at Harlequin.com.

CAST OF CHARACTERS

Detective Yara Thomas—Police detective.

Brandon West—Attorney and brother to Shawn, Ryan and James West.

Detective Martin Rachlin—Yara's police partner.

Tanya Rutger—Nurse and Brandon West's client.

Jasper Reinholt—Tanya's ex-boyfriend.

Dr. Anand Gristedes—Tanya's boss.

Chapter One

Detective Yara Thomas hadn't had time to grab a cup of coffee or boot up her computer before her lieutenant bellowed for her from his office.

So it was going to be that kind of day.

She stood in front of his desk as Lieutenant Ted Wilson gave her a brief rundown of the new case he was assigning to her. His exact words were, "Dead body in a car on old Route 30. Go."

She went.

Forty minutes later, she slowed around a curve and parked her standard-issue unmarked police sedan at an angle next to a police cruiser with its red and blue lights still flashing. Together her car and the cruiser created a barrier completely blocking the southbound lane of the road. A tow truck from one of the area towing companies that the department contracted had blocked the northbound lane. Not that anyone was traveling this stretch of the highway at night. The faster, better-paved and more centrally located interstate had long since enticed most of the traffic that might have made the trek down this dark, forlorn road.

A frigid wind blew as Yara stepped from the unmarked police sedan. She wore what she thought of as her work uniform—black slacks, a button-down shirt, blue with thin white stripes today, but the color and pattern varied from day to day, and black low-heeled boots. As usual her long, dark brown hair was pulled back in a tight, tidy bun. As a concession to the early November weather, she'd added a black pea coat to her usual ensemble along with a black knit cap, which she pulled down over the tops of her ears as she strode toward her sometimes partner, Martin Rachlin, who stood talking to a uniformed officer and another man. As she did, she made note of the scene.

A second uniformed officer stood guard next to a red Mercedes sitting on the side of the road, the driver's side door open. The plate read "Flyin'" and Yara couldn't help but wonder how many times the driver had been pulled over for speeding.

No flares around the car. The hood was closed. None of the three tires she could see were flat. No indication that the driver had stopped because the car had become disabled in some way.

If the car didn't break down, why had the driver chosen to pull over on this desolate road?

"What do we have?" she asked, stopping next to Martin.

Martin was a couple of inches shorter than her five-ten and outwardly self-conscious about his stature. He compensated for it by donning a tough-guy attitude that often grated on her nerves, although she did her best to be a team player and not show it.

Martin gestured toward the older man, who looked more than a little shell-shocked. Yara put him in his early sixties. Medium height, thinning brown hair, bushy eyebrows. "This is Nelson Freeman. He stopped when he saw the car to see if the driver needed help."

"I saw the blood and I freaked out. I called 911," Mr. Freeman said.

She gave the man what she hoped was a calming smile. "That's exactly the right thing."

He wrung his hands. "Maybe I should have tried CPR. Maybe she could have been saved if I'd tried."

She put a hand on the man's shoulder. "You did exactly the right thing. Sir, do you live around here?"

He nodded. "Yes, ah, my wife and I. I was on my way home from work this morning when I saw the car. I work security at an office building on the Upper West Side. The night shift. I prefer taking this side road because it's quiet. Only a few cars ever use it."

She glanced at Martin. "Do we have Mr. Freeman's statement and contact information?"

Martin nodded.

She motioned for the uniform standing near the Mercedes. She read his nameplate when he joined the group. Kilingham. "Officer Kilingham, can you make sure Mr. Freeman gets back to his car? Sir, you can go home now. If we need anything more from you, we'll be in contact."

The officer led Mr. Freeman away.

She turned back to Martin and the uniform he'd been talking to when she walked up.

Martin was older than her by two years but she'd joined the force right out of college and doggedly worked her way up to detective in only five years. Two years better than the average, but still a year longer than it had taken her older brother, Henry, who was now a sergeant with the San Francisco Police Department and, according to her other brother, Eddie, soon to be a lieutenant. Always the little sister chasing her smarter, braver, stronger big brother and not quite catching up.

Personal problems were for another day, so she forced her focus back to the present.

"Officer Connell." Martin jerked his head at the officer. "First on scene."

Connell had the buzz cut that so many of the young uniforms seemed to favor. As was her habit, she noted his stats—average height, dark hair and eyes, stocky, but not fat. May have been a wrestler in school. "Ma'am, my partner and I were first on scene. We arrived at 21:12 hours." Connell threw his shoulders back and met Yara's gaze directly.

She appreciated the show of respect. Too many of the guys on the force still held misogynistic views about female superiors even in the twenty-first century. It looked like Connell wasn't one of them.

"The car looked to be disabled," Connell continued.

"Was the driver's side door open like it is now?

Yara looked up from the notepad she'd taken from her pocket when Connell had begun talking.

He shook his head. "No, ma'am. I opened the door to ascertain the possibility of giving first aid. It was too late."

She made a note. "Okay, go on. The car appeared to be disabled when you got here…"

"Yes. I called in the tags and they were clear. I couldn't see it when I first pulled up, but as I approached the vehicle on the driver's side with my flashlight out, blood was visible on the window. I called for the driver and anyone inside the car to show their hands. When there was no movement from inside, I approached." He paused, swallowing hard.

Yara surmised it was his first time seeing a dead body. He looked young, but then all the uniforms were looking younger and younger these days. "It's okay, Officer Connell. Take your time."

Connell swallowed again before continuing. "I could see there was only one person in the car and that…she was covered in blood. It didn't look like she was breathing. I tried the door and it opened. She was slumped over the steering wheel. I could tell she was gone but I felt for a pulse. When I didn't find one, I called for EMTs and major crimes."

Yara nodded. "Good work." She jerked her chin in the direction of the tow truck. "Could you let the driver know we will be here a while yet."

Connell marched off to take care of the task.

Yara turned to Martin. "Have you taken a look yet?"

"Just a quick one. CSI has gotten all the photos

and the medical examiner's people are ready to move the body so we should be good to do a more thorough look-through. I figured you'd want to haul the whole car back to forensics and have them do their thing there."

"Sounds good."

She stuffed her notebook back into her coat pocket and followed Martin to the luxury sports car.

An air freshener shaped like a tree hung from the rearview mirror. It must have been pretty new because the smell of pine hung heavy in the interior of the car even with the open door.

A white woman, mid to late twenties, with blond hair now matted with crimson blood rested against the steering wheel. One arm hung on either side of her body, pink manicured nails sparkling. She wore a long, gray bubble coat and pink strappy heels. Her long pale legs were bare, but the hem of a pink skirt peeked through the opening where the two sides of her coat gaped open at her knees. Her head was turned toward the driver's side window, which made it easy to see the bullet wound in her right temple.

Yara's eyes traveled over the interior of the car. A gun lay on the console between the two seats next to the gearshift.

Suicide?

Possible. She didn't see a note but that wasn't unusual at all. Despite what people were used to seeing on television, most people who committed suicide did not leave a note explaining why they'd decided to take such an extreme, and final, step.

A purse lay on the floor on the passenger footwell. Yara stepped around to that side of the car and opened the door with a gloved hand. "Her purse is still here so that reduces the chances this is a robbery gone bad."

A look of confusion traveled across Martin's face. "Robbery? I'm surprised you're even considering it. This looks like a clear-cut case of suicide to me. Dark road. Gun in the car."

Yara grabbed the purse from the car and glanced at Martin over the roof of the car. Yes, she'd worked her tail off to make detective in record time, but one of the reasons that Martin had struggled with the same task, only earning his shield a little more than a year ago, was that he had developed the habit of jumping to conclusions.

"I'm considering everything until the evidence tells us otherwise."

Martin frowned but didn't say anything more. He was one of the men in the department who couldn't quite hide their displeasure with working with a more senior woman. Too bad. If she had her way, she'd always work alone, but the powers that be had determined that pairing detectives up was a good idea, at least in certain cases. Assigning two detectives to every case just wasn't feasible. She could only hope that Martin would catch his own case and leave her to work this one, whether it turned out to be a suicide or something more insidious, alone.

She pawed through the medium-sized Louis Vuitton bag that ran in the thousands of dollars. The car, the purse. Whoever this woman was, she had money.

Yara found the woman's wallet, also a Louis Vuitton and also costing a good chunk of change, and pulled out the driver's license.

"Name on the driver's license is Tanya Rutger." She bent down, looking across the vehicle's interior to compare the face in the driver's license photo with the one she saw on the other side of the car. "Looks like her."

She handed the license off to Martin and stepped back so he could do his own comparison. "She's twenty-nine. Lives in Manhattan." As she spoke, she went through the other items in the purse. "Has got lots of credit cards. Let's see. I've got an employee identification for the Stryder Medical Clinic. Same name as the license. Says she's a nurse there."

Martin straightened and handed Tanya's driver's license back to her. "My mother was a nurse. They must be making a lot more money than they made back in the day if Tanya can afford this car and a place in Manhattan."

"Don't forget the purse." Yara held it out in front of her. "It retails for a couple grand and the wallet is another grand."

Martin cocked an eyebrow.

"According to *People* magazine. I myself am a lowly public servant who can only dream of such luxuries. Hence the *People* magazine subscription and no Louis Vuitton."

Martin chuckled.

Yara frowned. "What do you think about Nelson Freeman? Is he involved in this?"

The man had seemed like a Good Samaritan just trying to do the neighborly thing and help a stranded motorist, but it wouldn't be the first time a killer had hung around the crime scene. For some it was part of the thrill.

Martin shook his head. "No. He seems credible. He was definitely shaken. Didn't detect any alcohol on his breath and he didn't have a record when I ran him. I think it happened just like he said it did."

She agreed with Martin's assessment. She'd take a look at Nelson Freeman but she didn't expect him to be anything more than a guy who was in the wrong place at the wrong time.

She crouched down, giving the interior of the car another once-over. The forensic guys would have a look for fingerprints on the gun and gunpowder residue on Tanya's hands but the blood-spatter patterns were consistent with someone sitting in the driver's seat and shooting themselves in the right temple. As best she could tell, there was no blood on the outside of the car, which would be consistent with a suicide.

What was so bad that you thought this was the best choice, Tanya?

That was the question. Assuming this was, as it looked, a suicide.

Something tickled at the back of Yara's mind. She opened the purse again. Wallet. Keys, probably for her apartment and maybe work. Lipstick. Half a dozen receipts. Earbuds. And a business card for Brandon West, Attorney at Law.

Her breath hitched. Why did her victim have

Brandon's business card? He was one of the best attorneys in town, which meant he was likely one of the most expensive. He also did mostly corporate work. So what would the victim, a nurse, need with a corporate lawyer?

Then again, the connection didn't have to be professional. It could be personal. Maybe Tanya and Brandon were seeing each other.

The thought wrapped around her chest and squeezed the air from her lungs.

She sucked in a deep breath and pushed thoughts of Brandon away.

"It's what I didn't find. What twenty-nine-year-old doesn't have a phone?"

Martin looked at her like she'd just sprouted a second head. "Every twenty-nine-year-old in the galaxy has a phone. I know some six-year-olds with a phone."

"Right. So where is Tanya's?"

"It's not in her purse?" Martin shined his flashlight in the back seat of the car.

"Not in her purse and not anywhere in the car that I can see," Yara said, following the trajectory of Martin's flashlight over the empty backseat area. Neither of them attempted to open the back doors. Searching for the phone wasn't worth potentially destroying evidence.

"Huh, well, maybe it slid under one of the seats. The forensics guys will find it if it's in there."

"I've got a faster idea." She dialed a number in her phone.

Detective Paris Vaughn answered with a, "Yo."

"Yo, yourself. Can you look up a cell phone number for me right quick?"

"Got a name?"

"Tanya Rutger." She gave Paris the home address, too, just in case there was more than one Tanya Rutger in New York City. It took a couple of minutes but Paris came back with a phone number.

"Paris found a cell phone number?" Martin said when she'd hung up.

"Yep, now let's hope it works." She dialed the number and put the phone on speaker so Martin could hear it ringing. She let it ring until the voice mail picked up. The recording didn't give a last name but they were told they'd reached Tanya, for whatever that was worth, which wasn't much at all.

"That doesn't mean the phone isn't in the car. It could have died or been damaged when she shot herself," Martin said. "Or if she may have just not wanted to take the chance of a friend or family member calling her and talking her out of what she planned to do."

Yara frowned. Not because he was wrong but because he continued to assume that Tanya Rutger had committed suicide. Working the case alone was looking better and better.

"Let's get a couple more uniforms out here to scour the area. Look for the phone and anything else that might be of value."

"Yes, sir." She knew the *sir* was not a sign of respect but she let it go. Martin's expression telegraphed his thoughts. This was a waste of his time. Tanya

Rutger had driven to a remote area and shot herself in the head. End of story.

Too bad for him she was the senior detective.

Yara headed back to her car.

"Where are you going, Thomas?" Martin called out.

Butterflies fluttered in her stomach. A missing cell phone wasn't the only loose end in this case. "To speak to a lawyer."

BRANDON WEST STOOD in a corner just outside the courtroom he'd just recently left with his client, Lakeisha Curtis. He hadn't been sure Lakeisha would show for the 9:00 a.m. hearing. This wasn't the first time she'd asked him to file a restraining order against her abusive husband. Each time she'd changed her mind before the hearing. But she'd not only shown up, she'd exhibited a resolve in the courtroom that morning that had renewed his hope that she was finally ready to leave her spouse.

He huddled with Lakeisha and her mother, making sure they were clear about the terms of the order and what they should do if her husband violated those terms.

Glancing up, he spotted a woman standing at the other end of the hall and his pulse raced.

Detective Yara Thomas of the Silver Hill, New York, Police Department. Her eyes were trained on him.

He took stock of the woman he hadn't seen in months but couldn't seem to stop thinking about.

Tall with a heart-shaped face, dark hair pulled back in a sleek ponytail, dark eyes that looked serious but not unkind and plump lipstick-red lips that appeared thoroughly kissable. Hot in a "could kick your butt" sort of way.

Maybe it was the gun.

The badge hooked on the opposite side of her belt said she was on duty. Probably visiting the courthouse on some official police business. His heart sank to his stomach at the realization that she was almost certainly not there to see him.

"Thank you so much, Mr. West," Lakeisha said, pulling his attention away from Yara. "The kids and I have moved in with my mother so you can reach me there if you need to. I haven't gotten a new cell phone yet. I'm changing my number so David can't keep calling me at all times of the day or night."

"That's a good idea. Be careful, though. I'm sure he knows you're at your mother's."

Lakeisha nodded and smiled. "Oh, he knows. But he won't come near there. He also knows my two brothers live with Momma and they'd just as soon shoot him as talk to him."

"Well, I hope it doesn't come to that. I've got to run, but you give me a call if you need me."

He turned and headed for the elevator without sparing Yara a glance and was surprised when she caught up with him as the door slid open.

"Mr. West, can I speak to you for a moment?"

So they were going formal. Well, he couldn't say she hadn't been clear about not wanting a personal relationship with him, so formal it was. Even if his heart was thudding in his chest like a snare drum.

It was early but the courthouse was buzzing with activity already. People streamed off the elevator.

He took a step back out of the way but kept his focus on the detective. "Detective, how can I help you?" He held the door and let Detective Thomas step onto the elevator before he did. Three other people were in the car going down with them.

"I was hoping to speak to you about a case I'm working on."

He searched his memory for a case of his that she could be working on. With the exception of the work he did with the women's shelter, most of his caseload was corporate work. Mergers. Buyouts. Loan facilities. While he was well aware that many corporate types were as criminally minded as any common gangbanger on the street, he did his best to weed them out during the extensive conflicts and background checks he did on each client before agreeing to representation. And since he had one of the country's premier investigative firms at his service, he hadn't had any trouble with the clients he chose to represent.

So what did the lovely Detective Thomas want with him?

"Well, I'm happy to help if I can." He emphasized the last word. If this was about one of his clients, he'd be bound by attorney-client privilege as to what he could tell the detective. "I only have a few minutes before I have to meet a client. How about I buy you a cup of coffee? There's a place on the corner that's good."

She bit her bottom lip, thinking.

Her hesitation irritated him further. "Or we can talk right here in the busy courthouse hallway."

"No, coffee sounds good."

The walk was short. The coffee shop was technically in the same building as the courthouse but had to be entered from the outside. He let Detective Thomas claim them a table, which wasn't hard to do. It wasn't quite 10:00 a.m. and most people hadn't yet felt the need for a coffee break or early lunch.

He ordered two regular coffees and two Danishes. He'd overslept that morning and hadn't had time to grab anything to eat before heading to the hearing. If the detective didn't want hers, he'd gladly take it.

Coffees carefully balanced on the plates next to Danishes, he made his way to the table. Yara was scrolling on her phone but when she saw him heading for her she dropped it on the table and rose to take one of the plates from him.

"Thanks. I wasn't sure I was going to make it."

One of Thomas's perfectly shaped eyebrows arched. "You could have asked for help."

"That would have been one way to go." He smiled. Asking for help wasn't exactly his thing. He was getting better at it, though. Or at least he thought he was.

Now settled across from the detective, he reiterated the question he'd asked her standing at the courthouse elevators. "So, Detective, how can I help you?"

"Do you know Tanya Rutger?"

His gut clenched. She worked major crimes and if she was asking about his client, it wouldn't be for anything good. "Yes. She's a client."

"And why did she need your services?"

That was the million-dollar question. He wasn't quite sure himself.

He'd met Tanya Rutger a week earlier. She'd been jumpy, obviously scared of something or someone. At first he'd thought she'd come to him on referral from the women's shelter. Most of the time the shelter's director, Joy Wynn, would call and make the appointment for the women at the shelter who wanted to file a restraining order against their abuser or, occasionally, initiate divorce proceedings. But not always. Many women stayed at the shelter for a very short period, sometimes as little as a night. Those women often came immediately after an assault, desperate to escape the violence. But a night in an unfamiliar bed surrounded by battered women—women they didn't see themselves in despite the similar bruises—left them feeling even more afraid. This was a life they didn't know. A future that was unsure. Most returned to their abusers figuring he'd have calmed down during the night. He was sorry. It had been her fault for being too loud, coming home late, talking back. And the cycle would continue.

Although she'd admitted to getting his name from a former client whom he'd helped escape an abusive relationship, Tanya hadn't been looking to file a restraining order, she'd made that much clear. What she did want to hire a lawyer for remained a little murky. She'd seen something that worried her, he'd gotten that much out of her. Something she was sure was illegal, but she hadn't known what to do about it. She wanted to make sure she was protected but she also needed time to think.

He hadn't been comfortable committing to represent her with such scant information but he'd allowed her to fill out the form he had all potential clients complete so he could make sure there were no conflicts of interest between a potential client and his current ones. And she'd insisted on leaving him a retainer with a promise to call him the following week and fill him in on the details of the case.

"Mr. West? Tanya Rutger? Why did she hire you?"

Under the circumstances, he felt it was best to keep his cards close to his chest. He leaned back in his chair. "You understand that attorney-client privilege keeps me from disclosing what my client and I spoke about."

She frowned. "I understand privilege."

"Then you know why I can't answer your question. Why are you asking me about Ms. Rutger?"

The look on her face answered his question.

"Tanya Rutger was found dead earlier this morning."

His heart sank. Though he hadn't really known Tanya, she'd seemed like an intelligent young woman who'd found herself in a tough spot. And now her young life was over almost before she'd really gotten a chance to begin it.

"I'm sure this has come as a shock, but it's important we get as much information as we can," Yara said. "I was under the impression you practiced corporate law. Has that changed since we last met?"

He smiled tightly.

"A lot of things have changed since we last met, Detective. But no, I still mostly practice corporate law. Occasionally, I take on cases outside of that area, though."

"When was the last time you spoke to or saw Tanya Rutger?"

The dismissal of his previous quest still rankled. For a moment, he thought about throwing out the privilege claim again but he suspected she knew the law, at least in this respect, wasn't on his side. When he spoke to his client wasn't a confidential communication. "About a week ago."

"In your office?"

His lips quirked up. "Yes, that is where I typically meet clients. West & Williams LLP does have two offices and typically clients find it easier to meet in the Lower Manhattan headquarters, but Tanya and I met in the Silver Hill office."

"Did she say why she wanted to meet with you there instead of in Manhattan?"

He shook his head. "She didn't. And I didn't ask."

Her frown deepened. "And you haven't spoken to her or seen her since?"

"No." Something was up and it involved Tanya Rutger. He wouldn't find out talking to Yara. Fortunately, he was related to a few people who could probably help him find out what was going on.

He dusted invisible crumbs from his hands. "I'm sorry, Detective. It seems we've reached the limit of what I can tell you about my client and, unless you're willing to share why you're interested in her, I have to be going now."

He stood and she followed suit.

"Thank you for the coffee and Danish," she said. "I'll be in touch."

Something to look forward to under any other circumstances but now, not so much.

She turned and marched from the coffee shop as if she had been the one to end their conversation.

Yara Thomas was a woman who liked to be in charge. Maybe it was time she learned to share the reins.

Chapter Two

Breathing seemed to come easier once she walked away from Brandon. She had managed to stay out of his orbit for the past several months but she hadn't anticipated how awkward it would be when she inevitably saw him again.

They'd met in this very courthouse after she'd spent a grueling day on the stand in a drug trafficking case. He wasn't one of the attorneys involved in the case, but he had caught some of her testimony and had complimented her after court adjourned for the day on having kept her cool under the defense attorney's barrage of questions.

Whether it had been fatigue or his chocolate brown eyes, she'd consented to letting him buy her a cup of coffee. And when he'd called the next day and asked to take her out to lunch, she'd agreed. A couple of more coffee dates and one very romantic dinner and she'd felt herself falling under the thrall of the handsome, successful attorney.

So she'd cut him off. Stopped taking his calls, returning his messages and texts. Cold turkey. Usually, if she got past a second date with a guy, she'd take him for a roll or two in the hay. A woman had needs, after all.

But even though there had been loads of sexual tension, like bucketloads, big hulking Mack truckloads of sexual tension, between her and Brandon, they'd never taken that step. And she had kind of liked it. Getting to know him on a deeper level and letting him know her a little more than she usually did with men as well. It had happened almost without her realizing it, but when she did, she put a stop to it right away.

She had a rule. No relationships.

They were simply too hard when one person was a cop. And it wasn't fair. Not when she could be hurt or worse.

It was better to keep things casual. And when you couldn't, to end them as quickly and cleanly as possible.

She called Martin on her way to the Stryder Medical Clinic and updated him on her brief and unfruitful conversation with Brandon. Twenty minutes later, Martin met her in the clinic's parking lot and they spent the next few hours questioning the two doctors who ran the practice and several of Tanya's coworkers. Word had already reached the practice about Tanya's death.

They spoke to the clinic's co-directors, Dr. Steven Manning and Dr. Anand Gristedes, as well as several other employees. Everyone said Tanya was a great employee and a good coworker, and though several people mentioned she had seemed somewhat preoccupied in the last couple of weeks, no one suspected depression or that she was suicidal. They all suggested they speak with Bailey Dunlap, a fellow nurse and Tanya's close friend. Unfortunately, Bailey had gone home, wracked with grief after finding out about Tanya.

She and Martin returned and they spent the rest of the morning finding out as much as they could about their victim.

Tanya Rutger rented a one-bedroom luxury apartment in Lower Manhattan, in a neighborhood where rents started at more than three thousand dollars and went up from there. When she and Martin arrived at the apartment around midafternoon, the building was quiet. Most of the residents were probably still at work slaving away to make their rent. She'd called ahead to inform the building manager of Tanya's death and the need to search her apartment.

A fortysomething woman in a conservative dark green suit and kitten heels waited next to the doorman's desk when she and Martin pushed through the revolving door into the lobby. The woman held a black-leather-covered folio and stood so straight Yara suspected the woman had spent time in the military.

"Detective Thomas?"

Yara extended a hand. "Yes. And this is Detective Rachlin."

"I'm Una Snowden, the building manager. We spoke on the phone earlier today." Ms. Snowden quickly shook each of their hands.

"Thank you for your cooperation," Yara said. She'd requested a search warrant for the apartment and faxed it to the building manager as a means of expediting entry into Tanya's apartment. She'd dealt with enough apartment managers to know that the real estate company would want the formal search warrant in order to cover themselves for letting the cops into a resident's home. Even a dead resident. Getting the warrant had taken longer than she'd have liked. There wasn't much urgency to an investigation when the victim appeared to have committed suicide, but the warrant had finally come through.

"Of course. Let me show you to the apartment." She led them to the elevators, which carried them to the sixth floor.

Tanya's unit was about midway down the long corridor of apartments.

Una unlocked the door and stepped aside.

Martin strode into the unit ahead of Yara, who hung back to question the apartment manager.

"When was the last time you saw Ms. Rutger?" Yara asked.

The other woman's forehead furrowed. "I don't have much contact with the residents unless they have a problem. Ms. Rutger was relatively new to our building. The last time I remember speaking to her was just after she moved in and I ran into her in the lobby. I asked her if she was settling in and she said she was. I don't think I've spoken to her since then."

"The warrant included the rental paperwork on the unit."

"Yes, I have that." Mrs. Snowden flipped her leather folio open and handed over a sheath of papers.

Yara flipped through them. The rental application was in Tanya's name and detailed a monthly rent of $4,300 a month. There was no way Tanya could afford that on her salary as a nurse, not even one working for a successful private practice.

"How did Ms. Rutger afford this place?"

"She was a nurse," Una said timidly.

Yara pinned the manager with a narrow-eyed gaze.

"There was a man with her. He didn't want to be formally listed on the application, but he said he would be paying the rent."

She studied the other woman. "And you allowed that?"

The woman shrugged, but her cheeks were beet red. "He paid the year up front. In cash. There was no risk on our end so I didn't see the harm."

A year up-front? She did the math in her head. That was almost $52,000. In cash. Not including any fees the building assessed. If this mystery man was throwing that much money around, he had probably thrown a little at Una Snowden to sweeten the deal.

"Did you get the name of this man?"

She shook her head. "No. He did not want his name connected to the apartment in any way."

Which almost certainly meant he was married and Tanya was his sidepiece. Since the apartment was in the financial district that could mean that he worked down here somewhere. At one of the many investment banks maybe? Of course, he could have chosen to set his mistress up as far away from his wife and everyday life as possible, which could mean he worked anywhere other than the financial district. The proverbial needle in a haystack.

"Do you think you could describe the man?"

The lines etched on Una's forehead deepened. "It's been months. I can't really recall. Average height and build. He had brown hair or dark blond, I think."

Her tone carried too much uncertainty for the description to be relied upon.

"Okay, Ms. Snowden. We'll let you know if we need you for anything further."

The manager let out a sigh of relief. Turning on her heels, she marched back toward the elevators.

Yara entered the apartment. She pulled a pair of gloves from her pocket and put them on. She could request a tech out to the apartment to lift fingerprints but she wasn't sure Lieutenant Wilson would approve it if the medical examiner came back with a conclusion of suicide. It might be the only way they'd find out who Tanya's mystery man was so she was determined to make the case for it. Right now he was one of the many loose ends she wanted to tie up.

The kitchen was small but functional. There was a dirty bowl and a glass in the sink as if Tanya intended to take care of cleaning up when she returned from work, but she'd never had the chance.

She opened the fridge. Veggies, milk, fruit, yogurt, eggs. It looked like Tanya had recently made a trip to the grocery store. Would a woman contemplating suicide bother stocking her fridge? She didn't think so.

She stepped into the bathroom, which like the rest of the apartment was pretty upscale. It had a prefab tub but tiles lined the walls around it and the vanity countertop was granite. A purple razor and a jumble of bottles—soap, perfumes, deodorant, nail polish, a cup holding a pink toothbrush and toothpaste—cluttered the vanity top. In the cabinet above the sink, she found hundreds of dollars of makeup and grooming utensils. A bottle of aspirin and over-the-counter allergy medicine were the only drugs in the medicine cabinet. Under the sink she found mouth-wash, body wash, lotion, feminine products, a hair dryer, flat iron and several curling irons. Nothing she wouldn't have expected to find in a twenty-nine-year-old woman's bathroom. Right outside the bathroom was a linen closet that held nothing but towels, sheets and other linens.

Martin stepped out of the bedroom a few feet down the hall. "Did you get anything from the building manager?"

She filled him in on the cost of the apartment and the mystery man who'd paid for a year up-front.

"And I'm guessing you want to find this guy even though this is looking more and more like a suicide."

She frowned. "We don't know what this looks like. That's why we are investigating, so yes, I'd like to talk to the man who paid for Tanya to live here."

He shook his head, the expression on his face saying he thought she was wasting her time. "Maybe he broke up with her. Maybe he was throwing her out of the apartment and she became despondent over losing her lover and her home. It happens."

"Tanya only moved in three months ago. The apartment was paid through for a year and in her name only. I doubt she could have been thrown out even if her guy had wanted to do so."

Martin crossed his arms over his chest. "So maybe the breakup was enough to drive her over the edge. We've both got a dozen more cases on our desk. Let's not turn this into more than it is."

She felt her frown deepen. His penchant for cutting corners was one of the reasons she hated it when Lieutenant Wilson assigned her and Martin to work together. "I'm not turning this into anything. I want to find the truth."

Martin rolled his eyes. "Well, I didn't find anything helpful in the apartment."

There was no way she was going to rely on Martin's search so she slid past him and into Tanya's bedroom.

The room was bright with light coming in through the open curtains. The room smelled faintly of strawberry and she recalled noting that the body wash, shampoo and conditioner Tanya used were strawberry scented. She scanned the space, taking in the neatly made bed and the shoes lined up on a rack next to what she presumed was the closet. The nightstand was bare of clutter holding only a single paperback, a romance. She opened the drawer in the nightstand. A power cord for a phone was coiled inside.

Tanya did have a phone. So where was it?

She stepped over to the dresser and opened the top drawer. Neatly stacked long-sleeved T-shirts and scrub tops were inside. Each of the remaining drawers was equally as organized and held nothing of evidentiary interest. She turned to the closet. Tanya sorted her clothes by type—shirts, dresses, skirts—hung side by side in a tidy row. The shelf above held sweaters and an assortment of jeans. Tucked below the hangers was a single silver roll-on suitcase with three more expensive handbags tucked away inside.

Out of everything she hadn't found in the apartment, the most conspicuous was the absence of a cell phone, computer or any other device. No way a twenty-nine-year-old woman didn't have at least a phone and a computer.

She returned to the living area and found Martin scrolling on his phone.

"There's not a single indication in this apartment that Tanya was distraught enough to want to end her own life," she said.

"Sometimes people don't show how disturbed they are to the outside world," Martin replied without looking up from his phone.

Maybe, but she didn't think that was the case here. No, the more she learned about Tanya Rutger, the less she thought the woman had committed suicide.

What then?

An accident seemed unlikely. So that just left… murder.

She had nothing more than a hunch, but it felt right.

Someone had killed Tanya Rutger and done their best to make it appear that she'd taken her own life.

The question was who would have wanted the twenty-nine-year-old nurse dead.

She couldn't help but think the answer lay with Tanya's mystery man.

Voices in the hall pulled her attention from her thoughts. She crossed the apartment and pulled open the door.

A woman was opening the door to the apartment directly across the hall with one hand and holding a cell phone to her ear with the other.

"Excuse me. I'm Detective Yara Thomas with the Silver Hill Police Department. Do you mind if I ask you a few questions about your neighbor Tanya Rutger?"

The woman's face morphed into an expression of concern. "I'll call you back," she said to the person on the other end of the line before dropping the phone in her open purse. "Is Tanya okay?"

This was one part of the job that she hated. "I'm sorry to have to inform you but Ms. Rutger was found deceased earlier this morning."

"Oh, my God." The woman slapped a hand over her mouth.

Yara gave the woman a moment to compose herself and pulled her notebook from her pocket before asking, "Could I get your name?"

"Ah, Sharon. Sharon Taylor."

"Ms. Taylor, did you know Tanya well?"

"Well, no. Just to say hello and make small talk if we were in the elevator together, you know? She was a pretty private person."

"When was the last time you saw her?"

"Last night, actually. She was on her way out when I was on my way in."

"And what time was that?"

The woman cast her eyes up to the ceiling. "Oh, about eleven thirty. I had a date. It went well," Sharon said absently.

"And did you talk to Tanya?"

"No." Sharon shook her head. "She seemed like she was upset and was in a rush. And she was on the phone."

So Tanya did have her phone with her last night.

She was already going to request Tanya's phone records but Sharon's details would help if she faced pushback from the lieutenant.

"Did Tanya have a lot of guests?"

Sharon shrugged. "Can't say I notice who comes and goes from my neighbors' places. We all pretty much keep to ourselves."

It was the blessing and the curse of living in the city. You could live side by side with someone for years and never really know anything about them.

"Thanks. If you recall anything that might help, please give me a call." Yara handed over a business card.

"Detective? You never said how Tanya died."

Yara looked into Sharon's anxious eyes. "I'm working on that."

Chapter Three

Detective Paris Vaughn had her long legs propped up on the seat of Yara's black desk chair. Seven months pregnant, she was on desk duty shuffling paperwork, running background checks and finding phone numbers for detectives in the field. And hating every minute of it.

"I don't think that's how ergonomic chairs work, Vaughn," Yara said, dropping her coat on the rack next to the door to the large room that housed four of the six detectives on the Silver Hill major case squad. The other two detectives shared a slightly larger office, two doors down on the same floor.

"It's working for me. At least for the moment. I've tried to tell this kid I'm doing him a favor, you know, letting him use my body to be birthed and all. The least he can do is go easy on me, but nooooooo."

Yara smiled across the desk at her friend. The fiery redhead was doing possibly the biggest favor one woman could do for another. After years of trying, Paris's older sister had been told that the chances of her ever getting pregnant and carrying a child to term were vanishingly small. Paris had volunteered to be her sister and brother-in-law's surrogate.

"You'll forget all these aches and pains the moment you hold your nephew in your arms." Yara rolled Martin's chair from his desk to hers and sat down.

"Don't you know it." Paris grinned. "I can't wait to meet the little guy. Did you find the lawyer?"

Paris had tracked down Brandon West for her at the courthouse.

Yara frowned. "Yeah, I found him."

Paris laughed. "Went well, then."

It was frustrating to say but Brandon had been the best part of the day even with his insistence on being unhelpful. The medical examiner refused to fast-track Tanya's autopsy. The cell phone company was taking its time pulling her phone records. And she had made no headway on finding Tanya's phone or the name of her mystery man.

"He wouldn't tell me anything else except that Tanya was his client."

"Well, I looked at her record when you were away. A single pop for disorderly conduct when she was nineteen. She hasn't had so much as a ticket since, so nothing there will tell us why she hired a lawyer."

"I'll find out one way or another." She smoothed a flyaway hair that had come free from the bun at the nape of her neck.

Paris's gaze was piercing. "Oh, ho ho. It looks like the lawyer got under your skin. I know I wouldn't mind getting under his—"

"Paris!"

"Sorry, sorry." She threw one hand in the air as the other rubbed her belly. "This pregnancy has got my hormones surging all over the place. That said, I have seen Brandon West. He was the defense attorney on a civil case that had a tangential connection to one of mine. He's smok'n hot."

Yara kept her eyes trained on the file in front of her. "I hadn't noticed."

Paris snorted. "Yeah, right."

Of course she'd noticed, but she had been very careful to keep her relationship—no, not relationship, the few dates they'd gone on—under wraps. Both because he was an attorney and because she'd only ever expected it to be a casual fling at best. That it hadn't even made it that far, well, she was glad she'd never mentioned the coffee dates to Paris or anyone else.

She glanced over the top of the file folder and caught Paris's amused expression.

"What?" she grumbled.

"Nothing. I just thought you should know that there was an incident report filed under Tanya's name. She reported a break-in at her apartment a few weeks back. The perps made a mess, but Tanya reported nothing of value was taken. NYPD responded. Tanya couldn't tell them who might be after her. The building only has security cameras in the lobby and however the perp got in it wasn't that way. There was nothing to go on."

Definitely not a B&E. There were much easier targets than a sixth-floor apartment, and in light of Tanya's death, she had to consider whether there was something to it. Maybe Martin wasn't wrong about Tanya having broken up with the boyfriend. And if he'd prepaid for a year's rent, maybe he felt justified in getting some of that money "back" by destroying Tanya's things. All great questions to ask the mystery boyfriend when she found him.

Martin entered the bullpen.

"Just got back from the lab. Only fingerprints found on the car and on the gun were Tanya's, the uniforms that were first on the scene and Nelson Freeman's."

Yara's ears perked up. "Freeman's? Did he mention touching the car in his statement?"

"No—" Martin shook his head "—and his prints were found on the outside of the trunk. I still don't see him being involved. You saw how shaken he was, Yar. He probably touched the car and didn't even realize he'd done it."

She frowned. More assumptions. "We need to follow up with him anyway. I pulled his record. It's clean. Let's go deeper. Talk to his neighbors. Friends. See if there's any connection at all between him and Tanya. Maybe they were having an affair."

Martin's eyebrows shot up. "A woman who looks like her doesn't date a sixty-something-year-old man. Hey, where's my chair?" His eyes skirted over Paris and narrowed.

"Just grab Jimmy's." Yara made no attempt to hide the irritation in her voice. "We both wondered how Tanya could afford an apartment in Manhattan, an expensive sports car and thousands of dollars in handbags. Maybe Freeman is her sugar daddy."

"Sugar daddy?" Martin plopped down in his purloined chair. "Did you read the background on Freeman? He's been married for thirty-nine years. Has two daughters and a grandson. Worked at the same place for forty-two years before retiring two years ago."

Yara sighed. "I'm not accusing the man of anything but we need to look into it. Forensics get anything else from the car?"

"No hair or fibers," Martin grumbled. "Still working on the blood spatter but so far it's all the same type so it's looking like it is all going to be Tanya's."

"Did they find a phone?"

Martin gave a thumbs-down.

No phone. That was the thing that bothered her the most. Everyone had a phone. Tanya had a charger for an iPhone in her night table, and her neighbor had seen her leave the apartment talking on her phone. So where was it?

Most people had their entire lives on the devices.

What was on Tanya's phone that someone didn't want them to see? And did that same someone kill her and make it look like a suicide?

There was no sign of anyone else in the car. That might be possible if the perp wore gloves and a hat. But how had he or she gotten away from the scene? The area wasn't exactly walking distance to anything.

There was also the question of how the killer had lured Tanya to the dark, desolate road so late at night.

She was a female city dweller. It was unlikely she was naive enough to take a drive down a dark road alone for no reason.

But if Tanya and Freeman were in some kind of relationship that could explain it. He admitted he frequented that road. Maybe it was their regular meeting place. Things got out of hand. Freeman ends up killing his mistress and then freaks out. Calls the cops.

Possible, but it was nearly impossible for Freeman to have killed Tanya in the heat of the moment and leave no forensic evidence at all.

She'd look into Freeman but she had to agree with Martin, he didn't fit.

"Thomas. Rachlin." Lieutenant Wilson strode into the bullpen. "Tanya Rutger's mother is here. I put her in the large conference room."

Martin groaned. "Sometimes I hate this job."

That was another thing she agreed with him on.

Chapter Four

West Investigations was housed in a three-story building on the Upper West Side of Manhattan. The interior was decorated in rich tones of deep beige and burgundy. Leather sofas and armchairs and tasteful abstract art decorated the waiting area.

James West Sr. had started West Investigations more than thirty years ago with work focused primarily on providing alarms and security systems for commercial buildings. Brandon's younger brothers, Ryan and Shawn, had expanded the business when they took over the day-to-day operations into a full-service security management firm that handled residential, commercial and personal security needs, as well as investigations of all types, for some of the world's most prominent businesses and individuals. While his older brother, James Jr., took on select investigative projects, Brandon had opted to keep his role with the family business firmly rooted in his expertise—legal work. He handled all the company's contractual business and served as their primary legal counsel, but left the security and investigative work to his brothers.

At least most of the time. A dead client seemed like a good reason to make an exception.

West's newest receptionist, Emily Kwan, greeted him with a wide smile as he strode toward the receptionist's desk.

"Mr. West, how nice to see you. Are your brothers expecting you?"

He smiled at the recent college graduate. "Emily, now, I've told you to call me Brandon. And no, my brothers aren't expecting me, but I'm hoping one or both have a moment."

"Let me just check." She reached for the phone, but before she raised the receiver, his youngest brother, Shawn, appeared from around the faux wall separating the reception area from the rear of the office where business got done.

For as long as he could remember, he and his brothers had been told how much they resembled each other and their father. The older they got, the more Brandon had to agree. Looking at Shawn now was like looking at himself five years ago. They had similar, medium brown coloring and dark brown hair and eyes, but his youngest brother was broader in the shoulders and sported a more muscled physique. His style was more casual and laid-back. Today, he wore dark jeans and a ribbed shirt under a dark sports coat.

Shawn's eyes landed on him and a boyish smile spread across his face. "Brandon. To what do we owe this surprise?" They shared a quick one-handed hug with a backslap. Shawn stepped back, his eyes roaming over the bespoke suit and black leather briefcase in Brandon's hand. "You're looking mighty serious. Are you here on business?"

"Actually, I am."

"Are we getting sued?"

Brandon quirked an eyebrow. "Not that I know of. Have you done something to get sued for?"

"If you don't know, I'm not telling." Shawn laughed. "Come on back."

He followed his brother back through the corridor, calling out greetings to the staff members who were in the first-come, first-served cubicles as he went. Private investigation and security work didn't lend itself to a typical office environment. Employees at West came and went as they saw fit, but the freedom to do their work without the boss unnecessarily hanging over their shoulders had created fierce loyalty in West employees. Most of the people who worked for West had done so for years, some having been with the firm since their father ran things. James Sr. had managed the company as if his employees were part of his extended family and Shawn and Ryan had continued the tradition when they'd taken over.

They finally reached Shawn's corner office, the walk having taken twice as long as it should have. Brandon wasn't surprised to find Ryan waiting in Shawn's office when they arrived.

"Took you long enough," Ryan said, looking up

from his phone. He sat in one of the visitor's chairs with his feet up on one corner of Shawn's desk.

"What can I say? Everyone wants to say hello to their favorite West brother," Brandon quipped.

He unbuttoned his suit jacket and sat on the black leather couch that formed part of the cozy sitting area in Shawn's office.

"In your dreams." Shawn knocked Ryan's feet from his desk and sat in his red-and-black high-backed leather executive chair behind his chrome-and-glass desk. "So what's the business that has you interrupting our very busy day here at West Investigations?"

"I need you to look into someone for me. A client of sorts."

"A client of sorts?" Ryan frowned.

"It's a long story. A woman came to see me. She was scared of something or someone but wouldn't give me details. She left a retainer so that's good enough for me to call her a client."

"Okay, so why do you need us to find her? Don't you have her contact information?"

"Unfortunately, she's dead. I got a visit from a major crimes detective earlier today."

He caught the look on Ryan's face. Months earlier, he'd told Ryan about Yara and that he thought he could develop real feelings for her. He was willing to admit he'd moped a little when she'd stopped taking his calls and he knew Ryan had noticed. There wasn't much Ryan didn't notice. But he hoped his brother would refrain from asking which major crimes detective had come to see him.

Thankfully, Shawn spoke first. "This is official, right?" He turned to face the computer monitor at the desk and began tapping on his keyboard, opening an official file, no doubt.

"All official. I'm hiring West as a consultant. As far as I'm concerned, Miss Rutger is a client until I'm informed otherwise by a representative of her estate." Bringing West on officially as consultants on Tanya's case meant that attorney-client privilege would also protect West's communications taken on his behalf.

"Tanya Rutger," Shawn said typing. "Address, phone number, social security number and whatever else you have. You know the drill."

He did, which was why he'd brought along a copy of the file he'd opened on Tanya Rutger. He took it from his briefcase and stood to hand it to Shawn.

"I'll scan all this info into the system later but for now…" Shawn typed furiously, no doubt pulling up all the information he could find on Tanya Rutger. It was why he'd come to his brothers. He did background checks on all his clients, before taking them on, but he didn't have access to the kinds of databases that West subscribed to.

"Could she have been involved with a violent partner?" Ryan asked.

"Tanya wasn't clear about exactly what her concerns were, but she wasn't looking to file a restraining order and I didn't get the sense that she was being abused. She dodged a lot of my questions at our initial meeting. I just know that she'd seen something that troubled her and she felt she might need a lawyer."

Ryan shot him a pointed look. "Whatever it was, it must have been big. You think she was involved in something shady or dangerous? Maybe she's on the run?"

"Maybe." But he didn't think that was it, either. That wasn't the vibe he'd gotten off her. What he'd gotten was abject fear. "I want to know what was going on. She was supposed to get in touch with me later this week, but she was killed before that happened. Why was she killed? What *had* she gotten herself into?"

Shawn looked over the top of his computer screen. "I can't tell you what Tanya Rutger is into but I can tell you about the new case the major crimes division caught yesterday. A body was found in a car on the side of a remote road earlier this morning." He turned the monitor so Brandon and Ryan could see it.

An article from a local news blog filled the screen. Under the headline "Dead Body Found" was a photograph of a red car being lifted onto the back of a tow truck.

He recognized the profile of the woman in the corner of the shot so he wasn't surprised by the probing look Ryan shot at him or Shawn's next words.

"Detective Yara Thomas is primary on the case. Was she the detective you spoke with?"

ENGROSSED IN WHATEVER he was reading on his phone, Brandon West didn't immediately look up when she entered the conference room, giving Yara a few precious moments to study the man. He wore the same suit he'd been wearing when she had met him at the courthouse that morning, but now he looked slightly ruffled. But ruffled worked on him. Hell, everything worked on him. It was the lean, wide-shouldered frame and expressive brown eyes that made her heart stutter when he turned them on her. The man was the definition of fine.

A faint warning bell went off in her head. She shouldn't be thinking of Brandon as an attractive man. Or thinking about him at all.

He sat in the chair with his shoulders hunched forward and frown lines creasing the skin at the edges of his mouth. She was good at reading other people's faces and body language. It was part of what made her so good at her job. And she knew Brandon West was worried.

After a moment, he looked up, finally seeming to realize he wasn't in the conference room alone anymore.

"Detective, I'm sorry. I didn't realize you had arrived."

She placed her notepad on the table and slid into a seat on the opposite side of the table from him. "It's not a problem. Can I get you anything? Water?"

He flashed a quick small smile. "That would be great, thanks."

She stepped out of the room and grabbed two bottled waters from the small kitchenette area at the end hall. She slid one across the table to Brandon and set the other one next to her notepad.

He twisted the top off the bottle and took a long sip, his Adam's apple bobbing.

"I must say I was surprised when the front desk clerk called to say I had a visitor," she said. "After our conversation this morning I didn't think you'd be cooperating with me."

He frowned. "I never said I wouldn't cooperate."

She shot a pointed look across the table. "Yet, you didn't cooperate when I asked for information."

"I have a duty to keep my client's confidence. I told you what I could given the circumstances then."

That sounded just like something a lawyer would say. Which was why they weren't her favorite people. Even the incredibly handsome, smolderingly sexy ones.

She mentally slapped herself and refocused. "And have the circumstances changed?"

"I think they might have. Tell me, is the body you found on the road this morning that of my client, Tanya Rutger?"

He set his phone on the table and turned it so she could see the article he had pulled up.

She swore under her breath. She'd thought the remote location would have bought them more time outside of the press's intrusive glare, but she should have known better.

She scanned the article. It didn't appear the vultures had Tanya's name, at least not yet. They would soon, Yara had no doubt. Thankfully, they'd been able to confirm Tanya's identity through her fingerprints and they'd already notified Tanya's mother of her daughter's death. The department media office was working on a press release as they spoke that was scheduled to go out later that afternoon but at this point there didn't seem to be much reason to keep Brandon West in the dark.

"I'm sorry to have to inform you, but the body we found this morning has been positively identified as Tanya Rutger," she said, falling back on her standard line for delivering news no one ever wanted to get.

Brandon let out a breath so deep it shook his broad shoulders. The sadness she saw in his eyes ran deep. He'd cared for Tanya Rutger.

An emotion flared in her chest but she'd have sooner taken a bullet than to call it out as jealousy.

"Were you and Ms. Rutger close?" She worked to keep her expression neutral, but flinched at how brittle the words came out.

If Brandon noticed, he didn't show it.

It would have been unethical for an attorney to get involved with his client but if he'd taken her on as a client because they had a personal relationship, that would explain how a nurse could afford his services. She'd done an internet search on Brandon West before their first coffee date months earlier so she'd known he had offices in Manhattan and Silver Hill before this case landed on her desk.

"Close as in personally? Not at all." He shook his head for emphasis. "I only met her once. A week ago, as I mentioned to you earlier, in my office."

The tension in her chest dissipated. She took a deep breath and got her thoughts back on track, on the case. "And you wouldn't tell me why she'd hired you."

"Couldn't and wouldn't aren't the same things. I'm not sure it would have helped you anyway."

Annoyance knotted her stomach. That wasn't up to him to decide. "Why don't you tell me and let me decide that for myself."

He gave a slight smile, revealing dimples in his cheeks that made her knees go weak. Good thing she was sitting.

"I'm not here to aggravate you, Yara. Once I realized that Tanya might be the poor woman you found this morning, I decided it was in her best interests if I provided you with whatever help I could."

Yara clicked her pen to ready mode. "I'm glad you made that determination. So, why did Ms. Rutger hire you?"

"I'm not sure exactly."

She knew what she'd been expecting him to say but it wasn't that. How could he not know what he'd been hired to do? Her face must have said what she was thinking because he held up a hand as if warding off her question before she could ask it.

"I know it sounds a little weird. Let me start from the beginning. Ms. Rutger came to my office in Silver Hill a week ago yesterday. She was visibly anxious about something and, though she didn't actually say this, I suspected she was more than a little bit afraid, which would have explained why she wanted to meet in Silver Hill rather than at the Manhattan office where I normally meet clients."

"Afraid? Afraid of what?"

He shook his head. "I don't know. She was very evasive in her answers to my questions. All she'd tell me is that she'd seen something illegal and that she thought she might need an attorney, but she wouldn't go into specifics."

"And you took her case without knowing what it was she wanted you to do for her?"

Most of the lawyers she came into contact with were either criminal defense lawyers or prosecutors but Brandon did not practice criminal law as one of his areas of specialty.

"My firm does a little of everything. Including my partner and I, there are ten lawyers at the firm and a dozen paralegals and support staff. We're a small firm with varied practice. It's how we survive the industry's ups and downs. I do mostly corporate work—mergers, acquisitions, loans, securities. But I also do a lot of pro bono work with women who are victims of domestic abuse. I thought maybe whatever she'd seen had something to do with that. While I don't normally take on clients without knowing the specifics of their representation, this was an unusual case."

She was surprised. Not many attorneys of his stature would do pro bono work on behalf of abused women. It made her like Brandon West more, and that was dangerous, because she already liked him a lot. Too much.

"Okay, so you thought Tanya might be a victim of domestic violence?" She jotted the letters *DV* on her notepad.

"I didn't say that. It's just that she gave off the same vibe as the women I represent. The same waves of fear and desperation. It's why I took her on without knowing exactly what she wanted from me. She was so upset about something, I couldn't just turn her way. She signed the retainer agreement and was supposed to contact me this week to discuss details. If her issue wasn't something that fell into one of my specialties, I would have made sure to connect her with an attorney in my firm that did specialize in her issue. Or, if need be, connect her with a firm that would take her on."

"Do you have any idea who referred her to you?"

He shook his head. "There's a spot for that on the intake form, but she left it blank. She did mention that she got my name from a friend who used my services in a domestic violence case, but I don't know which client. I don't usually push if a prospective client doesn't want to answer that question. They have their reasons."

Brandon might not have been sure about the domestic violence theory, but it was a possibility she'd have to explore. Especially given what she knew about Tanya's mystery man. Although public perception of domestic violence usually centered on lower-income and marginalized women as the primary targets of abuse, she knew that far more middle-class and upper-income women were victims than

anyone wanted to admit. Tanya's expensive car and
apartment might be explained by a boyfriend, maybe
one who was abusing her? But Tanya's mother hadn't
given them a lot to work with. She hadn't thought
Tanya was seeing anyone and she hadn't been to
Tanya's new apartment. To be honest it didn't seem
like mother and daughter were particularly close,
although the woman had been devastated to learn
of her daughter's death. It wasn't unheard of for an
abused woman to hide the abusive relationship from
their family and close friends.

"Okay," she said, going back through the notes
of the conversation she'd had with him earlier in the
day. "And you said you hadn't spoken to her since
that day in your office. Was that the truth?"

She looked up to find his face stormy.

"Detective Thomas, the rules of my profession
may not allow me to tell you everything I know, but
I do not lie."

She saw that he was genuinely angered by her
implication that he'd lied to her. "I'm sorry. Let's go
back a step. The last time you spoke to Miss Rutger
was a week ago, correct?"

"Yes," he bit out. "Last Tuesday to be precise. The
day she came to my office and I began the paperwork
to formally begin our professional relationship. I did
leave a message for her a couple of days after that,
last Friday, asking her to call and set up another appointment so I could get more information on what
she wanted me to do for her, but she never returned
my call. After speaking with you this morning, I

tried calling her again but, of course, there was no answer."

"You tried calling her on her cell phone?"

"Yes. It's the only number she gave me. Why do you ask?"

"We didn't find Ms. Rutger's cell phone with her belongings."

His eyes narrowed. "She definitely had a cell phone. She had it in her hand the entire time she was in my office. When she filled out the intake form, she used it to pull up information."

"What do you ask on your intake form that she needed to look up on her phone?"

"Just information on next of kin and close relatives. I have to make sure that the interests of any new clients don't conflict with the interests of any of my current clients."

Yara nodded her understanding. "Can you give me the number you called and any other contact information you have for Ms. Rutger? I want to make sure it's the same as what we have for her." She turned to a clean sheet of paper and slid her notepad across the table to him. "I also wouldn't mind having that client intake form and your notes from the meeting with Ms. Rutger."

He glanced up from writing with a wry smile. "Nice try, Detective."

She felt herself smile back. "It was worth a shot."

He copied Tanya's information. When he was finished, he slid the notebook back to her. "Can I ask you something?"

It was unlikely she'd answer, but she was curious about what he wanted to know. She gave him a little nod. "Go ahead."

"The article said you'd found Tanya's body in her car on the side of the road. It didn't look like there was any damage to the car, at least not from the photo in the article. You're a major-case detective. Can I take it that Tanya didn't die of natural causes while driving?"

She instinctively rebelled against telling him anything about an open case, but the press release would be out any minute stating that Tanya Rutger had been shot.

"Tanya didn't die as a result of a car accident. She was shot."

His eyes widened and he jerked away from the table a little, as if trying to put more distance between himself and the information she'd imparted. "Shot? As in murdered?"

She shook her head. She didn't need him getting ahead of her investigation. "We don't know that. Not yet. We are investigating the case as a suspicious death at the moment." Another piece of information that would be shared with the public in the press statement being released.

"What is the other option?" His brow furrowed in thought. "Suicide? You think she could have shot herself?" He shook his head. "I don't think so. I know I only met her in person once, but Tanya Rutger didn't strike me as suicidal."

"You said she was very worried about something."

"Yes, she was. And scared if I read her right. But if she was planning to commit suicide, why hire me?"

"I don't know. Maybe she didn't start contemplating suicide until after she left your office."

"You think it's possible she went from scared but hiring a lawyer to suicidal in a week's time?" He shook his head, disbelief written over his face.

She agreed it wasn't likely, but as he'd said, he only met her once and only briefly then. He couldn't possibly say for sure Tanya wasn't suicidal when she'd walked into his office.

"I assure you, I will be investigating all possibilities, Mr. West."

He sighed. "Yara, given the situation, I think we can put aside the awkwardness from our brief prior association. Just call me Brandon."

Prior association. Something about categorizing whatever they'd started months earlier so coldly stung. But if he could move on, so could she.

"Sure, Brandon." She gave a tight smile. "Let me walk you out."

Chapter Five

"Police found the body of a woman parked in her car off of Interstate 95 yesterday morning. Details remain scant, but authorities say that Tanya Rutger was found having suffered at least one gunshot wound. The case is being investigated as a possible homicide. It's time for us to take a short break, but when we return Dan Coates will be here with your five-day forecast."

Brandon used the remote to turn off the television, then powered down the stationary bike he'd been cycling on in his home gym.

Ryan and Shawn lived in New York City, but he'd bought a townhome in the tony suburb of Silver Hill, New York, less than an hour from Midtown Manhattan. It was ironic. Both Ryan and Shawn were married. Ryan had a young daughter and Brandon was sure that Shawn and his wife, Addy, would be adding to the West clan any day now. But both of them had elected to live in the city while he, the single, childless brother, had purchased a two-thousand-square-foot townhome in the suburbs. His brothers loved to tease that he was the most married unmarried man they'd ever met.

He didn't mind the teasing. He'd known from the first moment he'd stepped into the house that he had to have it. The first floor boasted an open-floor-plan kitchen that flowed into the dining room, which in turn flowed into the living area that looked out onto a backyard where he'd lovingly planted roses, hydrangeas, lilies and any other flower that caught his fancy. As a boy growing up in a three-bedroom apartment in Harlem in a concrete city, he'd dreamed of one day having a home that he could spread out in, with each room having one primary purpose, and a backyard where he could run around with a dog. The hours he worked kept him from having the dog, but he'd made sure his home fulfilled every other requirement. The large master suite was his sanctuary, the place where he relaxed and let all the stress of his job go. There were two additional guest rooms and a small room he'd turned into his home office. On the lower level of the three-level home, he'd set up his man cave and used the last bedroom as his home gym. It was perfect.

He moved now from the gym to his office, stopping in the gourmet kitchen to refill his water bottle with filtered water. He slid behind his desk and opened an email from his investment adviser. He'd done dual graduate degrees at Columbia, earning his law degree and his MBA at the same time. It had seemed prudent given his intention of going into corporate law, and in the years since he'd graduated and started practicing, it had paid off several times over. Understanding the world of finance had made him a wealthy man, independent of the money he made practicing law, and it meant he didn't have to think twice about working with the domestic violence shelter and taking on clients who couldn't pay his usual hourly fee.

A quick scan of the email from his adviser told him that he was in no danger of falling into destitution anytime soon. He clicked out of the email and into the secure system the firm used. West & Williams LLP had two offices, one in Lower Manhattan and a second in Silver Hill. Last year, he'd taken on his sister-in-law, Addy Williams-West, as a partner and she ran the office in Manhattan like a well-oiled machine. He had an office in the Manhattan space, which he visited when he needed to, but he spent most of his time in the Silver Hill office staffed by one associate and paralegal. It was a setup that worked for him.

An email waited from Shawn. Brandon had called Ryan and Shawn after his talk with Detective Thomas and confirmed what they'd already suspected. The body found earlier that day was his client's. Ryan hadn't seen a purpose in continuing to dig into Tanya's past, but Brandon had insisted and Shawn had agreed to take on the project himself. He'd attached everything he'd been able to pull up on Tanya as of five that afternoon and promised to keep digging.

Shawn had only been on the case less than a day,

but the report he'd sent was characteristically thorough. Tanya Rutger had been born and raised in Hackensack, New Jersey. After graduating from high school, she'd earned her nursing degree and certifications. She'd worked in a number of places before landing a job with Stryder Medical Clinic, a private medical practice on the Upper East Side. The report listed her address and phone number as the same ones she'd given on the intake form. Shawn had also noted that Tanya didn't appear to have a roommate and that the typical one-bedroom apartment in the luxury building she lived in started at three thousand dollars. Very pricey for a nurse. There was a Mercedes sports car registered in her name. Another pricey item, not just because of the cost of the car, but add in the cost of renting or buying a parking space in Manhattan, gas and insurance and it was clear, without even knowing how much she made, that Tanya was living well above the means of a nurse.

What were you into, Tanya?

He skimmed past the photos of the various social media posts that Shawn had included. He'd read them before the night was over. Social media was always a gold mine, but if there was anything in particular that stood out above the rest, Shawn would have called his attention to it. Instead he moved to the section of the report titled Criminal Record, Reports and Proceedings.

Tanya's criminal record was clean; he knew that from the background report he'd had done on her. What the standard report hadn't turned up, and why he'd gone to his brothers, was an incident report filed on Tanya's behalf. Three weeks before her death, someone attempted to break into her apartment.

Irritation churned in his chest. Detective Thomas had undoubtedly known about this incident and hadn't told him of it. Of course she hadn't. They weren't a team.

Emotion swirled inside him at that thought. Something primal. Yara's repeated failure to respond to any of his messages or texts after their third date was a clear "uninterested" signal. He was not the type of man who pursued a woman who didn't want to be pursued. But he couldn't deny she'd gotten under his skin in those three dates.

He wasn't even sure how she'd done it. She was prickly and short-tempered. She took herself far too seriously and she was a cop for goodness' sake. He should be glad she'd blown him off. But he wasn't. He'd tried dating other women to get over whatever she'd done to him but it hadn't worked. He still thought about her months after their brief relationship had ended.

He didn't need this right now. He needed to focus.

Her job was to find Tanya's killer. And his job was to…?

He wasn't sure anymore. He had no idea what Tanya had wanted him to do for her and it didn't matter now anyway. Why was he spending precious billable hours on a case that had no living client?

Because Tanya Rutger hadn't deserved to die the way she had. Alone. On a dark road. Shot.

He didn't believe for one second that she'd committed suicide. The young woman who'd hired him had been upset, yes, but suicidal? Not a chance.

Whatever situation Tanya had found herself in, it most likely had led to her death. She'd come to him for help and that's what he was going to provide.

He turned back to the incident report. The apartment had been broken into, but according to Tanya, nothing was stolen. The place had been destroyed, however. The sofa cushions had been slashed as had the clothes from Tanya's closet. Food had been thrown on the kitchen floor and walls. The mirror in the bathroom shattered. These weren't actions of a typical burglar who was most concerned with getting in, grabbing a few valuables and getting out before anyone was the wiser. The cop had noted as much, stating in the report that the incident appeared personal, but that Tanya had sworn that she had no angry ex-boyfriends or other enemies who would destroy her home.

But someone had done just that. And three weeks later she'd come to him, terrified.

It had to be related.

The question was, how?

It was a question he was determined to answer.

He grabbed his phone and hit the speed dial for his brother. Shawn picked up after two rings.

"I got the report you sent. Thanks for getting on this so fast."

"No problem. It seemed like a priority for you."

"It was. Is. Listen, could you look into the break-in at Tanya's apartment some more? Since nothing was taken, I know it wasn't a priority for the cops."

"It's likely to get another look now, though."

"I know, I know, but Detective Thomas is not going to tell me anything so I need to do this myself."

There was a long silence on the other end of the phone.

"Do you think you might be getting too involved with this case? I get that she was your client, but this really is a police investigation now. Getting involved, for you and for West Investigations, could have consequences."

"I don't want you to do anything that would jeopardize the firm in any way. It's just that Tanya came to me. She was worried and scared and I agreed to help her."

"And you would have if she hadn't been killed. You have nothing to feel guilty about."

"It's not guilt exactly. I don't know what it is. I can't stop thinking that if I'd pushed her a bit harder on why she wanted to hire a lawyer, maybe I could have done something. Maybe she wouldn't have been killed."

"My sources are saying it's looking like a suicide, Brandon."

"It wasn't." He heard the forcefulness in his tone and tempered it. "It wasn't. I talked to Tanya a week before her death. She was not suicidal."

Shawn sighed. "Okay. I'll see what I can find out and get back to you."

He hung up the phone, still thinking about Shawn's

words. What was driving him to look into Tanya's death? Obligation? A savior complex? If that was it, he was too late.

He wasn't sure what it was, but he knew he wouldn't stop. Not until he knew why the scared young woman who'd come into his office a week ago was lying on a slab in the morgue now.

And who had put her there.

THE SILVER HILL Police Department's forensics division occupied a two-story warehouse about a twenty-minute drive from the main police headquarters. The lower-level garage served as a workspace for evidence that was too large to process in the lab. Tanya's red Mercedes was parked at the rear of the large space.

Becca Chandler worked at a desk next to the door. "Detective, welcome to my humble abode."

"You don't live here."

"Well, it sure feels like I do sometimes."

"I get that. I got your message. I hope you've found something in the car that I can use because right now I've got a whole lot of nothing."

Becca grinned. "I've got something." She tapped an empty plastic bag on her desk. "Bad news first. I found this caught in the locking mechanism on the back right side of the door."

Yara stepped closer to the desk and peered at the bag more closely. That's when she noticed it wasn't empty. A small scrap of black material just a little wider than a piece of thread.

"Since this is the bad news, I'm going to guess you didn't find blood or DNA on it."

"That would be a good guess. It's clean."

Yara thought back on the scene. "A pink skirt, white blouse and gray coat. That's what Tanya was wearing when we found her. Nothing black."

"Well, I can't even tell you how long the material had been there, but given its size and its precarious placement, I'd say not too long."

"Okay, but a scrap of material is not going to be much help unless we can tie it to someone."

"That's why I called it the bad news, although *bad* is not exactly right." Becca crooked her index finger. "Follow me."

Yara followed her to the car. All four doors were wide open. It had been too dark when they found Tanya and the car to get a good look at the interior. Under the harsh bright lights of the warehouse, the crimson was a shock against the expensive beige leather of the seats.

"As you can see—" Becca pointed to the front passenger area "—most of the spatter was concentrated in the front right side of the car. That's consistent with your victim sitting in the driver's seat and being shot in the right temple."

Yara felt her stomach drop. "So you're saying it was suicide."

Becca wagged a finger. "Not so fast." She moved from the front of the car to the rear seat. "See here and here." She pointed to a spot of blood on the back right door and another on the midsection of the back seat.

"Yeah, more blood, but wouldn't you expect some to get in the back of the car?"

"I would. But what I wouldn't expect is for there to be a big break in where it landed."

"A break?"

"There's blood on this side window and on the leather seat here but nothing in this area between."

"No blood at all?"

Becca shook her head slowly. "Not a drop."

Yara tingled with anticipation.

"Taken with the material I found on the door…" Becca paused.

Yara finished the thought. "Someone was in the car with Tanya Rutger when she was shot."

Chapter Six

Florence Rutger still resided in the Hackensack home where she'd raised her two daughters alone after her husband walked out on her twenty-three years earlier. Shawn hadn't done a deep dive into Tanya's mother's life, but his report had revealed that Florence Rutger was a retired school bus driver, avid Powerball player and devoted churchgoer.

Brandon parked in front of the one-story home, walked up the concrete walkway and rang the doorbell. The buzz of the television ceased abruptly, replaced by the sound of heavy footsteps heading for the door. The white lace curtain covering the window in the door was pulled back by a round-faced man in his mid-twenties.

The man peered out at him with suspicion. "Yes? Can I help you?"

"My name is Brandon West. I'm an attorney who was hired by Tanya Rutger. I was hoping to talk to Mrs. Rutger about her daughter."

The man let the lace curtain fall back into place. For several long moments nothing happened. Brandon could see him on the other side of the door and hear murmuring voices inside but he'd angled away from him, talking to someone he couldn't see in the house. He was beginning to think he wasn't going to be let in when the locks tumbled and the door opened.

The man wore a forest green sweat suit and running shoes. "Now is not a good time for Ma to have visitors. There's been a death in the family, and…"

A female voice came from farther inside the house. "Nick, I said to let the man in."

Nick's face pinched and he gave Brandon a dark look before holding the door open just wide enough to let him slide through. As he did, the man whispered, "You best not upset her. She's been through an awful thing these last twenty-four hours."

Brandon looked into the man's eyes. "I know and I'm sorry. I have no intention of upsetting her. I want to help."

His statement did nothing to remove the suspicion from the man's expression.

Brandon walked through the narrow foyer and into a living room. The floral scent in the small space was nearly overwhelming. Flowers covered every surface in the room. A tiny woman sat on a large floral-patterned sofa. Or maybe she just seemed tiny. Grief circled her like a vulture. Her eyes were bloodshot and she clutched a tissue in her hand.

"Mrs. Rutger, my name is Brandon West. I'm an attorney. Tanya hired me before she died."

"Please have a seat," the woman said in a low voice. She waved him toward the armchair across from the sofa. "And please forgive my son. He's protective of me."

Nick, still giving Brandon a wary eye, sat on the couch next to his mother, wrapping an arm around her shoulders.

Florence Rutger wore a colorful blue-and-white caftan and matching head wrap. The resemblance between her and Tanya was striking. Tanya had been the spitting image of her mother, only thirty or so years younger.

"Thank you for seeing me at a time that I know must be extremely difficult for you. And let me just say how truly sorry I am for your loss."

Nick huffed. "If you know how difficult it is, why did you come?"

"It's all right, Nick." Florence patted her son's hand absently. "You said my Tanya hired you, Mr. West?"

"Please, call me Brandon. Yes, about a week ago Tanya retained me to represent her."

Surprise flashed across Florence's face. "Represent her with what?"

Brandon scooted forward in the uncomfortable armchair. "To be honest with you, Mrs. Rutger, I don't exactly know. I was hoping you could help me with that. We only met once and Tanya said she'd seen something illegal and she thought she might need a lawyer. She seemed afraid and said she needed a little more time before she could tell me more but that she wanted to make sure she didn't get into any trouble. Do you have any idea what she could have been talking about?"

Florence shook her head. "No. None at all." Then her eyes turned sad. "Tanya and I hadn't been getting along well in the last few months."

"If you don't mind my asking, why was that?"

"And if she does mind," Nick snapped, "why are you so interested anyway? You cops spoke to my mother yesterday and asked a bunch of questions. I know you think Tanya committed suicide, but there's no way."

Brandon wished he could talk to Florence alone, but since that didn't seem to be on the menu, he opted for placating her son. "I'm sure the police are doing everything they can to get the answers you deserve. That's all I want as well. Tanya came to me for help and even though she's no longer here, I want to help her."

"Nick, would you be a dear and make a pot of coffee, please. Oh, and Darlene bought that apple pie. Would you heat up a few slices, please?"

Nick shot a look at his mother that made it clear he knew that she was trying to get rid of him. But he rose, doing a sideways shuffle between the couch and the coffee table, and headed for the kitchen.

"I'm sorry," Florence said, keeping her voice low. "Nick is very protective of me at the moment. He won't leave my side, even though there's nothing I want more right now than for everyone to just leave me alone with my grief."

Brandon couldn't help feeling like a heel. The woman had just lost her daughter. He should have waited at least another day or two before barging in and asking questions. "Maybe I should go. I don't want to add to your grief."

He started to rise, but she waved him back down into his seat. "No. No. Tanya came to you. She trusted you and you want to help. Nick is right about one thing. The police seem to think Tanya killed herself. I know she and I were going through a rough time of late, but I know my baby. She would have never killed herself. Never. And the way..." She pressed the tissue to her eyes and guilt kicked him in the gut again.

"Mrs. Rutger, do you remember the names of the officers who questioned you yesterday?"

The sound of a cabinet slamming came from the kitchen followed by the tap coming on.

Florence dabbed at each eye one last time before lowering the tissue. "Ah, there was a male and a female. Thomas and Martin something. I remember the man's first name was Martin because he said it, like, with a French accent. Mar-teen, not Mar-ten. He was also the one who seemed intent on saying Tanya committed suicide even when I told him that there was no way."

Knowing that Detectives Thomas and Rachlin were headed toward writing Tanya off as a suicide assuaged some of the guilt he felt for ambushing Florence. If the cops weren't going to do their jobs and investigate thoroughly, he would.

Time to get this interview back on track. "Why weren't you and Tanya getting along?"

Florence sighed. "Tanya has been going through something lately. She wouldn't tell me what. I get it.

She is…was twenty-nine. A grown woman, but I'm still her mother and I could see something was eating at her. She and Jasper had broken up some months ago so I thought that might be it, but when I asked her about it, she told me that she'd broken up with Jasper and that it was amicable."

He pulled his phone from his pocket to take notes. He could hear the coffee maker bubbling in the kitchen. They didn't have a lot of time before Nick returned. "What's Jasper's last name?"

"Reinholt. Jasper Reinholt. He's an assistant professor in the anthropology department at NYU."

"When did they break up?"

Her eyes tracked to the ceiling as if she was thinking. "About six, maybe seven months ago."

"Did Tanya ever have any problems with him? Did he ever hurt her?"

"You mean, like, did he hit her? No, never. Jasper wasn't that type of guy. He loved Tanya. I'd hoped they might marry and give me some grandbabies one day, but then Tanya just announced they'd broken up. Said he wasn't the one for her."

"Tanya was a nurse. I know that they aren't always paid well. Did she ever have money problems?" Based on Shawn's report, Tanya was living well above her means so it wasn't so much as she didn't have money, but that she seemed to have money that couldn't be accounted for. He was working his way up to the questions that might have Florence kicking him out of her house, but he had to have answers.

She hesitated a beat too long for him to accept

her subsequent answer as truthful. "No. No money problems."

"Mrs. Rutger, I only want to help Tanya. I know she was driving an expensive car and living in a luxury apartment downtown. That seems well out of reach of a nurse's salary."

Florence glanced over her shoulder into the kitchen. From where Brandon was seated, he couldn't see Nick, but the racket that had been coming from that direction had died down considerably. She turned back to face him.

He could sense her holding back and decided to press a little harder. "Mrs. Rutger, the police look like they plan to close Tanya's case as a suicide if they can. I met Tanya. I don't believe she committed suicide. The more information I have, the more likely it will be that I can convince the cops to keep investigating her case."

Florence's gaze dropped to the tissue in her hand. "I didn't tell the police about this when they came. I thought maybe if they saw what a good person Tanya was, they'd rethink their silly theory about suicide."

"I understand." It wasn't uncommon for people to paint loved ones in a favorable light after they'd lost them. Even loved ones they hadn't been all that fond of while they'd been living.

"Tanya and I argued over the car and the apartment," Florence said. "I don't know exactly how she paid for it, but I suspected it was a man."

"A man? Jasper?"

Florence's laugh was without mirth. "Definitely

not Jasper. Like I said, he's an assistant professor. He had Tanya and I over to his place in the Bronx for dinner once and, well, I ate to be polite, but his place should have been condemned as unfit for habitation by man and beast."

"Okay, not Jasper, then. Is there anyone else you can think of who could have been paying for her new lifestyle?"

Florence shook her head, wringing the damp tissue in her hands until it tore into two pieces. "I don't know. I really don't, but she moved after she started her new job."

He recalled the employment section of Shawn's report. "With the Stryder Medical Clinic, right?"

"Yes, she was so excited." A smile bloomed on her face, then fell just as quickly. "She moved into that new apartment and bought that fancy car. I worried that she was overextending herself. I knew the new job paid more than her old one, but she was spending so much so fast."

"Did you ask her about it?"

Florence nodded. "She got mad at me. Told me she was grown and knew how to manage her money. And she did. Tanya was always very good with money, but still. I'm not so old that I don't realize how much things cost."

"What did you suspect?" He had his own suspicions so he wasn't surprised by her answer.

"I thought she was dating a rich, married guy. Lord knows there are plenty of them in New York City. I asked her point-blank whether she was letting some man pay her way. Told her I hadn't raised her like that. That's when she stopped speaking to me." Florence tore the tissue into smaller and smaller pieces that landed on her lap.

"And you have no idea who this man could be?"

Florence pinned her gaze on him. "I have no idea if this man exists, Mr. West. Tanya didn't take my calls for a month after our argument. When she started speaking to me again, I didn't want to drive her away so I let it go. I figured if…when the relationship with the man went south, she could always come back home and live with me if it came to that." She looked at him with eyes filled with tears. "I should have kept asking questions. I should have made her tell me. Now she's gone and I may never have answers."

Chapter Seven

The office was empty when Yara got back from the forensics lab. She tossed her suit jacket over the back of her chair and woke her computer, still thinking about the implications of Becca's findings. The medical examiner had emailed his preliminary report while she'd been driving back to the station and she was eager to see if his findings added anything to the evidence they'd collected so far.

The phone on her desk rang.

"Thomas. My office. Now." It looked like the ME's report would have to wait. She shrugged into her suit jacket as she made the short walk from her shared office to his corner one.

His door was open. She knocked on the door frame before striding in.

"Have a seat." Lieutenant Wilson pointed to the pair of visitor's chairs opposite his desk without looking up from the paperwork on his desk. Wilson was a former college football player, many years removed from his playing career, but he'd done well keeping in shape. Large in stature and personality, he was affectionately called a curmudgeon by some in the department while others held far lower opinions of the man.

Yara fell into the latter camp. Wilson worried too much about the bureaucracy and the politics that came with the job and not enough about the job itself, as far as she was concerned. He had his eye on moving up the ranks and he wasn't about to let little things like fairness or justice get in his way.

Half a minute passed before he took his reading glasses from his face and sat them primly on top of the report he'd been reading. "I saw the medical examiner's preliminary report on the dead woman you caught yesterday. Looks like a suicide just like Rachlin said."

She sucked in a harsh breath. Martin shouldn't have been saying anything to the lieutenant about a case she was the primary detective on. Especially, when he knew she disagreed with his rush to judgment.

"Sir, I'm not convinced this is a case of suicide. I just got back from forensics and there's some evidence that might suggest someone was in the car with Tanya Rutger when she was shot."

One of Wilson's eyebrows arched. "What evidence?"

"A small piece of material was found on the right rear passenger door and gaps in the blood-spatter pattern suggest the possibility that someone was in the back seat."

"That's hardly conclusive." He slid his glasses

back onto his face and looked at the computer screen on his desk. "The ME says the head wound is consistent with the victim shooting herself. I understand the only prints on the gun found in the car were the victim's, correct?"

"Yes, sir, but there are other circumstances that also make me think that there is more to this case."

Wilson pinned her with a look. "Such as?"

"I haven't been able to find the victim's phone. It seems peculiar to me that a twenty-nine-year-old wouldn't have her phone on her. Nor was I able to find it at her apartment."

"She could have lost it. It certainly has no bearing on the medical examiner's finding that the wound is consistent with suicide."

Irritation bubbled in her chest. She wished she'd had time to read the medical examiner's report before Wilson called her into his office. She would have been better prepared.

Lieutenant Ted Wilson had risen up the ranks quickly due more to his political savvy than any outstanding achievement in police work. What he understood better than most was that perception was the key to reality. A high case-close rate for the major case division fed into the police commissioner's tough-on-crime persona and boosted the lieutenant's political aspirations. And that in turn boosted Wilson's professional cache. Wilson wasn't shy about telegraphing his desire to one day sit in the commissioner's seat. Having the current commissioner and the mayor indebted to him would help get him there.

"That's one explanation. It's also possible some-one was in the car with Tanya and they took it."

"You don't even know there was anyone in the car. A scrap of material and the absence of blood are not enough to make a case."

Her jaw tensed. "I'm aware of that, Lieutenant. The victim also appears to have been living outside of her means. Fancy car. Expensive apartment. I'd like to find out who exactly was paying for her lifestyle. That might help give a fuller picture of who Tanya Rutger was and whether she was actually suicidal."

Wilson pulled his glasses off again and threw them on the desk in front of him. It was his signa-ture move, a show of irritation. "Detective Thomas, you have nearly a dozen open cases on your desk at the moment, am I correct?"

He knew he was correct. No doubt he'd checked the system to see just how many other cases she had before he'd called her into his office.

"Yes, sir."

"So digging around in, what for all accounts, looks like a straightforward case of suicide, would not seem like the best use of your time."

"With all due respect, I wouldn't call it digging around. I'm pursuing all possible leads so that we can assure the Rutger family that no stone was left unturned."

"You spoke to the family?" At her nod, he con-tinued. "Did they give you any indication that the woman was afraid of anyone? In some kind of trou-ble that might have led to her death?"

Frustration churned in her stomach. "No."

"What about friends? Neighbors?"

"No. She had hired a lawyer, though. He said she seemed worried about something. That she'd seen something illegal and thought she might need an attorney."

"Well, if she was mixed up in something illegal, that could be her reason for committing suicide. It wouldn't be the first time a criminal took the easy way out."

"Yes, but the lawyer said she'd seen something illegal, not that she was involved in it."

He shot her an incredulous look. "If she was close enough to illegal activity to see it, she was most likely involved in it. Maybe she lost her nerve."

She had to fight the urge to reach across the desk and smack him. That was the kind of attitude among some law enforcement that got innocent people railroaded into jail. You were there so you must have been involved in the crime somehow. Funny how that same logic never seemed to apply to the bankers, corporate CEOs and politicians who were perpetually unaware of what was going on right under their noses.

Wilson leaned forward and tapped a finger on the papers covering his desk. "Detective Thomas, unless the medical examiner or forensics people come back to you with some new evidence that conclusively puts someone in the car with your victim, this is a suicide. I don't have enough time or resources to let my detectives run around turning over rocks in the faint hope of finding a crime."

"Sir—"

"Thomas, this case is not a priority. I've already released the woman's apartment to the management company so they can notify the mother she can clear out the place. I've assigned Rachlin to another case. It's time for you to move on." He snatched his glasses from the desk, his focus now back on the papers in front of him. It was clear she'd been dismissed and she didn't like it one bit.

Her blood boiled. "Sir, with all due respect, releasing the apartment was my call to make as the primary on the case."

Wilson peered at her over the top of his rimless lenses. "Everything that goes on in this station is my call to make, Thomas. And I made it. The owner of the building called this morning complaining that the seal was unnerving to the other residents and causing unnecessary stress to people in their own homes. You already said you didn't find anything of evidentiary value there."

There was something else going on here. Seven years as a detective had honed her instincts enough that she knew when something was off. She'd look into it when she got back to her desk, but she wouldn't be surprised to find out that the owner of the building was well connected. Whoever it was would have to be to make it in New York City real estate.

She'd worked under Wilson for the last four years. She knew when his mind was made up. He'd decided

Tanya Rutger was a case of suicide and wasn't worth his detectives' time and she wasn't going to change that opinion today. But maybe she could at least get him to allow her to track down the phone.

"What about the phone? It's a big loose end. Can I at least request the call and GPS records from the phone company? If you're right and she just lost the phone along her daily route to work, I could find it and wrap up the loose end."

Wilson glared but she could tell he was considering it. After a moment he said, "Fine, but your workday needs to be focused on closing the string of robbery cases you have on your desk. That's your priority until it's closed."

She had four cases of break-ins at homes in an upscale part of Silver Hill and the local media had started to take notice.

"Yes, sir," she answered through gritted teeth.

She rose and headed for the door. Before she got it open, Wilson spoke again.

"And Thomas? The mayor has taken an interest in these robbery cases. Citizens having their homes invaded is not good in an election year. It's in your professional best interests to get your priorities straight and focus on what matters."

Florence Rutger had only hesitated a moment when Brandon asked if he minded if he took a look at Tanya's apartment. She gave him the spare key that Tanya had given her and promised to call the doorman to let him know that she was sending someone over to collect some of Tanya's belongings. He didn't know if the detectives had sealed off Tanya's apartment and he wasn't willing to go as far as breaking a police seal in his quest for answers. He'd never liked driving in the city so he headed home and called the car service the firm kept an account with. He checked in at the office while he waited for the car, and a half hour later he was on the way to Lower Manhattan.

Florence was good to her word. The doorman let him up to Tanya's sixth-floor apartment without delay. There was no notice warning that the apartment had been sealed by police order, so he slid the key into the lock and let himself inside. Tanya's one-bedroom wasn't spacious and its only view was of the neighboring apartment building, but the kitchen appliances were brand-new, the fixtures were high-end and the floors were marble tile. Apartments might have started in the thousands of dollars a month, but whoever was paying for this place was shelling out quite a bit more than that.

"What did you get yourself into, Tanya?" he whispered.

The police report on the break-in had stated that the place had been torn apart, but in the three weeks since the incident, Tanya had made great strides with the decor. A dark brown suede sofa anchored the living room and a round glass-top table took up most of the small eating area. The walls, free of decor, and the faint smell of paint lingering in the air were the only signs that there had been anything amiss in the apartment recently.

He made his way to the bedroom. A queen-size sleigh bed was flanked by nightstands on either side. Tucked into the corner by the en suite bathroom was a five-drawer dresser.

He'd always been careful to keep his work separate from his personal life. And this, well, it was definitely not separate. It felt intrusive being in a client's bedroom even with Florence's permission to look through Tanya's things. But it seemed inconceivable that Tanya could have been seeing a married man, one willing to pay for an apartment like this, and there be no hint of who he was in her apartment.

He opened the drawer in the bedside table and looked through the items inside. A notebook with a few vague comments about dreams. Pens, a box of checks and a few other things that held no interest to him. There were a few business cards scattered in the drawer, as if they'd been thrown inside without much thought. He laid them on the bed and took a photograph just in case. He doubted she'd have kept her lover's business card. Why would she? But stranger things had happened.

He made a mental note to stop by the management office and see if he could find out who was on the lease. No doubt that a man who went as far as setting a woman up in a fancy apartment knew better than to put his own name on the lease and the management company probably wouldn't tell him anyway, but there was no harm in asking.

He bet Detective Thomas already knew the answer. Had it made her more or less sure Tanya had killed herself?

The other nightstand was empty.

He closed the drawer and headed for the closet, wondering if a place like this did a full walk-in or one of those deals where, yes, technically you could walk in if there were no clothes hanging inside and you were no bigger than the average twelve-year-old.

He was reaching for the knob when the door flew open, banging into his head and sending him reeling backward.

Before he could catch his breath or get his footing, a fist slammed into the side of his face that the door had missed.

Stars swam behind his eyes, but he managed to stay on his feet. His vision blurred but he was still able to see the malice in the brown eyes that stared out at him from behind the black ski mask.

He shifted his weight, avoiding another roundhouse punch, and charged his attacker, grabbing the man around the waist and driving into the wall next to the bed.

The man let out an *ooof*, then another when Brandon's fist connected with his jaw.

It wasn't his best showing. His head rang from the two blows.

The masked man feinted left, avoiding the next punch, then launched his own, catching him in the stomach.

Brandon doubled over, all the air having left his

body with the gut punch. The intruder pushed him aside and ran for the front door to the apartment.

Footsteps pounded. The creak of the door opening and slamming shut. Then nothing. The apartment was utterly quiet.

It took a few more minutes before his lungs were working properly again. He didn't bother chasing after his assailant. Whoever had been in the apartment was long gone.

Instead, he pulled his phone from his pocket, glad he'd never erased Yara's phone number.

Chapter Eight

Yara strode into the apartment, her expression a mixture of irritation, exhaustion and concern. Brandon sat on the sofa, an ice pack on the bump on the side of his head where the closet door hit him courtesy of the EMTs who'd come and gone after he'd refused transport to the hospital. He watched as her gaze swept over every inch of the space before landing on him.

His heart raced and his body heated.

Now he listened as the detective got an update on the situation from the officers. The assault hadn't merited dispatching a New York City detective to the scene, but she had immediately taken charge, ordering the officers to gather the security tapes from the building management. The officers scurried to do as instructed and Yara turned her attention to him, her fashionable but functional black boots clicking against the tile floors.

"Brandon." She looked him over, her expression one of distinct displeasure.

"Yara." He lowered the ice pack and pressed his

fingers to the bump, measuring its width. It didn't seem to be too large, thankfully.

"You want to tell me what happened here?"

He sighed. He knew when he called her and told her what had happened, she wouldn't be happy with him.

He gave her the quick summary of how he'd come to the apartment to see if he could find anything that might point him in the direction of who might have wanted to hurt Tanya and how a man in a mask had jumped out of the closet.

Yara took notes as he spoke. "Did you see any identifying features?"

"Not much. He was a couple inches shorter than me, maybe five-eleven, six feet. I could see enough of his skin around his eyes to tell that he was white. He was wearing gloves. And he had brown eyes."

"Clothing?" she asked, still writing.

"Black pants. Black shirt. Black mask."

"Shoes?" she said, looking up from her notebook finally.

He closed his eyes and tried to bring the memory of the man into focus. He hadn't really been concentrating on anything other than not getting hit in the face again, but when he'd been hunched over after taking the punch to his gut his gaze had been trained downward.

"White sneakers. Can't tell you a brand, sorry."

"No, that's good. Now tell me, how did you get into the apartment?"

"Tanya's mother gave me permission and a key."

He pulled it from his pocket. "I didn't break in. And come to think of it, I don't think the intruder did, either. I mean, the door was locked when I arrived. I used the key, and it didn't seem like the lock had been tampered with, although I guess you guys can check on that."

Yara's expression darkened. "Whoa, wait a minute. You went to see Tanya Rutger's mother?"

He didn't care for the feeling of her hovering over him like a displeased parent, so he stood. The upward motion sent a stab of pain ricocheting through his already throbbing head. He winced.

"Sit down," she snapped, placing a hand on his arm. Despite the bite to her words, her grip was gentle as it guided him back onto the couch. Once he was back down, she sat next to him.

One of the uniformed officers returned, interrupting them.

"Detective Thomas, the management is pulling the video for you. They'll email it to you."

"Great. Thank you, Officer." The man retreated into the hallway.

"Now, you were explaining why I shouldn't arrest you for interfering in my case."

He smiled despite himself. He always had liked strong women and everything he'd seen of Yara Thomas said she didn't suffer fools easily. "I went to see my client's mother. To express my condolences and to see if I could make any sense of why Tanya hired me in the first place."

"And did you?"

"Yes and maybe. Tanya's mother told me that she believed Tanya had begun dating a man who she suspected was married and paying for Tanya's new lifestyle."

Yara's back stiffened. "Her mother didn't mention anything about a boyfriend when my partner and I questioned her."

"She admitted she hadn't told you. She said she felt like you and your partner had already made up your minds that Tanya had committed suicide. She was afraid if she said anything it might make it seem more likely that her daughter took her own life."

Yara swore and stood. She paced to the bar separating the kitchen from the living area and turned around. "To be clear, I do not believe Tanya committed suicide. I can't say the same for my partner or my lieutenant, but I have not written this case off as suicide."

Maybe Yara could be an ally after all. "I'm glad to hear you say that."

She held up her hand. "Unfortunately, my lieutenant does not share my belief. He thinks this is a clear-cut case of suicide and he wants me to focus my attention on my other cases. He's already released the apartment, which is the only reason you haven't been arrested for breaking and entering."

He pushed to his feet now, the pain of doing so dimming in the face of his outrage. "How can he do that? I mean, Tanya had someone break into her apartment only three weeks ago. That alone should raise suspicions that there's something other than a suicide here. And now this guy attacks me in the same apartment."

Yara's eyes narrowed. "How do you know about the break-in?"

There was no reason to hedge. "I got my brothers to do a bit of research for me. There's no one better at finding out things people would rather keep under wraps."

She shook her head, curiosity and disbelief at war in her expression. "Why get so involved in this case? I get that Tanya was your client, but you'd met her once and didn't even know what she wanted from you. Is it guilt? Obligation? A hero complex? What? Why not just let it go?"

"I don't know, and trust me, I have asked myself the same questions." He rubbed his throbbing temples. "Maybe it's a little of everything. Maybe it's just that no one was there for Tanya when she needed it most and it cost her everything. I can't save her life, but I can save her reputation. I can make sure that if she was killed, her killer doesn't get away with it."

Yara cocked her head to the side, studying him.

He didn't know her well enough to read her expression, but he suddenly wished he did. Seeing her again despite everything reminded him of how much he'd liked spending time with her. She was the only woman he'd dated since his divorce he could say that about. But now wasn't the time to explore those thoughts.

"I don't think I'm the only one who can't let this

case go," he said. "Your lieutenant ordered you off the case, so why did you come when I called?"

She frowned. "I wish I knew. Maybe I'm a glutton for punishment."

"I'll tell you what I think. I think you're not the kind of detective, the kind of woman, who would let an injustice go unsolved if she can help it."

She studied him intently for a moment. "The New York City cops were happy to let me step in here because you weren't seriously hurt and there's a connection to my case, but my boss was clear. If I push this, I'm putting my career on the line."

He threw up his hands. "Even now? It's obvious that guy was here looking for something. Something that might point to why Tanya was killed."

Yara shook her head. "If my lieutenant can close this as a suicide, he will. It's quick and it doesn't impact his crime stats. Plus—" she hesitated for a moment "—there's the medical examiner's report. He found Tanya's wound was consistent with a self-inflicted gunshot to the head."

A lead balloon landed in his stomach. "I don't buy that."

"Whether you buy it or not, my lieutenant does and he's in charge ultimately."

Brandon shook his head. "Not of me, he isn't. Whoever broke in here was looking for something. What? And why? It seems to me Tanya had something that someone wanted enough to kill her for, but for some reason they still haven't found whatever it is so they came back to search for it here."

Yara threw her hands in the air. "Look, there's nothing I can do."

He closed some of the distance between them and stared into her eyes. "That's not true. Your lieutenant can officially order you to focus on other cases, but he can't tell you how to spend your free time. Help me. Help me find out the truth about what happened. Suicide. Murder. Whatever."

She shook her head slowly, but he could see the wheels turning in her head, the interest behind her eyes. "Do you know how hard I've worked for my career? I don't want to stall out at a detective's rank."

"You share whatever you feel comfortable sharing. The truth is, I'm going to investigate anyway, and between me and my brothers, I can probably find out anything you don't give me. It would just take me longer, which would give Tanya's killer more time to cover up and get away," he pressed.

Yara's frown deepened into a scowl, but her eyes were thoughtful.

"This is going to happen one way or the other. But this way we can build a rock-solid case that you can take to your lieutenant and that he can't ignore. Maybe that will help when—if—there's blowback from you having pursued the case in spite of his order."

"You don't know Lieutenant Ted Wilson at all." Yara laughed without mirth.

But he could see it in her eyes before she said the words. She was in.

"This has to stay quiet. You and your brothers know about my involvement and no one else."

"Absolutely, partner." He stuck out his hand.

Yara hesitated for a millisecond before taking his hand in hers. He saw the electric shock that ripped through him at her touch reflected in her eyes.

She dropped his hand and took a step back.

"I didn't find anything before the attack, but I'd only just gotten started. I want to take a more thorough look around."

"I don't know what you think you're going to find. I searched this place after we found Tanya's body. There was nothing here that led me to a boyfriend or anyone else of particular interest, for that matter." She followed him into the bedroom.

"You never know. With more information, maybe things will look different now. Something might stand out."

But after twenty minutes, it was clear there was nothing in the apartment that pointed to Tanya's secret boyfriend. Which was in and of itself a clue.

"You know, if Tanya was rendezvousing with a secret boyfriend here, she went to great pains to erase any sign of him," Brandon said.

Their search had moved from the bedroom to the living spaces. Yara closed a kitchen drawer she'd been searching, and turned to face him in the living room, where he'd methodically removed the couch cushions and searched every inch of the sofa.

"I was thinking that maybe they'd broken up. That

maybe the boyfriend was the person who broke in three weeks ago and trashed the place," she said.

"Out of anger or revenge." He turned the idea over in his head.

"Or both."

"Maybe. I'm sure you asked the management for the names on the lease."

"Just hers. And the rent was paid each month by an automated payment from an account in Tanya's name only."

"So if someone else is paying for the apartment, they are making sure to cover their tracks," he said, putting the couch back together having found nothing.

"I have to get back to my neck of the woods before my lieutenant starts asking questions. Maybe we can meet up later to exchange information?"

He liked the idea of seeing her later more than he wanted to admit to himself. He was going to have to keep reminding himself that they were only working together. But maybe… "Absolutely. Why don't you give me a call when you get off your shift."

"Okay. How about you? You need a ride?"

"I can find my way home."

She looked at him as if he'd just bumped his head, which, technically, he had. "You have a huge bump on one side of your face and a shiner on the other. If you get behind the wheel, I will have the city cops pull you over and take you in for reckless driving."

"Don't worry, Yara. I don't think I could drive even if I wanted to, not with the hammering going on in my head. I took a car here and I'll get one back to Silver Hill."

And he wanted to stop by West Investigations' offices and update Shawn on the situation anyway.

Yara gave him a small smile. "Okay, well, until tonight, then."

The words sent a flutter through his stomach. "Until tonight."

Chapter Nine

Yara spent the rest of the day working the robbery cases and debating whether she was putting herself on the path to career ruin by helping Brandon West. She almost certainly was. Lieutenant Wilson wasn't the type of man who admitted to ever being wrong. Bringing him conclusive evidence, if she found any, would more likely be seen by him as a direct challenge to his authority rather than as an industrious detective going the extra mile. And yet she knew she couldn't let this case be closed as a suicide. Not with all the loose ends she saw just hanging out there.

It had been a very long time since she'd left work on time, but when the clock struck 6:00 p.m., she logged off her computer and grabbed her coat. Martin was out in the field and Paris had left early for a doctor's appointment. The other detective who shared the office was engrossed in a phone call and didn't look up as she strode from the room.

In her car, she started the engine before pulling up the contact in her cell phone for Brandon West. She tapped her foot while she waited for him to pick up. She was inexplicably nervous, as if she was fifteen calling a boy she had a crush on. Not that she had the courage to call a boy at fifteen, especially one who was as cute as she guessed Brandon West would have been.

Adolescence had been a decidedly painful time for her, most notably because her mother passed away during that period of her life. Her grief-stricken father and two older brothers hadn't had the first notion about how to shepherd a young girl through the thorny patches to womanhood. She'd done the best she could, mostly relying on the wisdom of her teenage girlfriends. And she'd turned out all right. At least she thought so.

"Hello." The low tone of the male voice coming from the other end of the phone line pulled her from her thoughts.

"Hi. Ah, it's Yara. I was just calling to see if we are still going to meet up this evening."

"Of course. Would you like to come to my place?" he asked.

To his house? She'd avoided that step during their brief dalliance and she wasn't sure that was a good idea now. "Oh. That's nice, but…"

He interrupted. "I'm trying to take it easy after my harrowing experience. And it affords us privacy."

Privacy was important. She thought about how Martin had spoken to Wilson about his suicide conclusion behind her back. She couldn't afford to have him or another one of her coworkers catch her out with Brandon West and report back to the lieutenant.

It would bring an onslaught of questions she wasn't ready to answer.

"What's your address?" she asked.

He rattled it off. "I'll order Chinese. Anything in particular you prefer?"

"I'll eat anything."

"I shall get a variety, then. See you soon."

His voice slid over her skin like velvet and she shivered before hanging up and backed out of the parking space. The address he'd given her wasn't far from the station, about a fifteen-minute drive, but she got caught in a bad patch of after-work traffic that drew the trip out to nearly half an hour. Her luck changed, however, when she turned onto his street. A car was pulling out of the space in front of the address he'd given her. She parked and followed the red-brick-paved walkway to the arched front door of the town house.

She pressed the doorbell and heard it ring inside the house. Moments later the door opened and Brandon West stood before her. He was dressed casually in jeans, a gray sweater and a well-loved pair of loafers without socks. The bump on his head seemed to have gone down a bit, but his black eye had moved from its early greenish hew to a dark purplish-black color. He was still breathtakingly handsome. So much so that she couldn't stop the tiny gasp that escaped her mouth.

The sexy smile that slid across his face sent her pulse racing.

"Perfect timing." He stood back and held the door

open so she could enter. "The food got here thirty seconds before you did."

"How are you feeling?"

"Not too bad. Better than I look, at least."

He looked pretty good to her but she refrained from making that comment aloud. "Did you ice your eye?"

"I did. Don't worry."

She followed him past a floating staircase and into an open-floor-plan kitchen, dining and living space that looked as if it should be in a magazine.

"Wow. This is incredible."

"Thank you. I fell in love with this place the moment I saw it."

She could see why. The kitchen was well apportioned with eggshell-white cabinets and granite countertops. Very modern but he'd toned down some of the modernity by adding a dark brown farmhouse table big enough for ten in the dining space and a deep, incredibly comfortable-looking sectional in the living room off the kitchen. But for Yara, the *pièce de résistance* was the wall of windows looking out onto the back patio and yard.

"I don't think I'd ever leave if I lived here," she said.

"I have to go to work to afford it, but it is nice to come home to each day."

She left him pulling white boxes out of the large brown bag and floated over to the six-foot colorful abstract painting on the dining room wall. It had caught her eye the moment she'd walked into the space, as it was supposed to, but she was still stunned to see the signature in the bottom right corner. "This is a Gerhard Richter."

Brandon turned to her with two plates in his hands and a look of surprise on his face. "You know your art. It is. I bought it some years ago before the rest of the world realized what a genius he is."

"I met him once. A long time ago." She couldn't take her eyes off the piece. "I minored in art history in college and he came to campus to speak. I'd seen some of his work in one of the SoHo galleries. I can't even remember which one now, but you're right, he's always had something, an eye for color and form that is so unique."

Brandon carried the plates to the table. "It seems we have at least one thing in common, then. We both love art."

"I don't know how we missed that before."

"Well, you stopped answering my calls before I could offer to make you dinner." He said the words lightheartedly, but they still sent heat crawling up her neck. He'd planned to make her dinner. Would they have ended the night with dessert in bed?

She'd have probably gone for it. Heck, she was thinking about it now.

"Yara, would you like red or white with dinner? Or both? You are off duty, correct?" he asked, pulling her thoughts away from the bedroom.

A laugh bubbled in her throat. "I am, but I'm not a big drinker. Let's start with white and see where the night takes us."

She hadn't meant for it to sound as flirty as it had.

She knew he'd caught the innuendo by the rise of his brow, but thankfully he only grinned before making his way to the fridge.

She fanned at the heat rising in her cheeks while his back was turned. She'd better be careful or this partnership might turn romantic, and she couldn't let that happen.

She cleared her throat and sat at the table. "So the management company at Tanya's apartment sent me the security recording. A guy matching your description came up through the stairwell in the parking garage to the apartment. Since the garage also allows public parking, we can't limit our pool of suspects to those who had access to the garage." She piled moo shoo pork onto her plate. "He also anticipated the cameras. Had the ski mask on before he entered the garage. The cameras caught him leaving, but it was the same deal. His face was always covered."

"Damn." He set a glass of white wine next to her plate and took the seat next to her, the spicy smell of his cologne tickling her nose and stirring a feeling in her nether region.

Platonic. Professional. She repeated the words several times in her head before speaking again.

"I think it might be worthwhile if you take a look at the recording anyway. Maybe it'll jog something in your memory that could help."

"Not a problem. I made a copy of the file my brother put together for you," he said around a bite of food.

She took a sip of wine before speaking. "You

know, your family has quite the reputation. West Investigations is one of the best firms for private security and high-end investigations. I was able to dig up a partial client list and to say it was impressive is an understatement. Basically, who's who of America's wealthiest people."

"Well, I am proud of the company my father and brothers have built. I'm not involved in the security and investigations portion, though I do manage their legal portfolio."

"Your reputation is nothing to look down on, either. Howard undergrad then Columbia Law. Three years in the prosecutor's office then seven years at Farrington & Barr, one of the country's biggest law firms, I might add. But then you chucked it right before you would have been made a partner at the firm and hung out your own shingle. Why?"

"I wanted something of my own. I'd worked so hard to make partner and the closer I got to it the less I wanted it. At least not on the terms that I would have had to accept if I'd stayed at Farrington."

"I have to say I don't know if I could have walked away after putting in all that time and effort."

"It didn't feel like walking away, though. It felt like starting anew." He grinned. "Does that sound corny?"

"A little, but I think I know what you mean." She laughed.

"I'm sure you do. It's why you're here. Why you're pursuing Tanya's case despite the possibility of harm to your career from doing so."

She looked at him, confused. "It is?"

"Certainly. You're not the kind of cop who only cares about pushing the papers and closing the cases. You care about finding the truth. About getting justice for victims, or at least as much justice as the system will allow. You wouldn't have made it as far as you have if you didn't."

"You got all of that in forty-eight hours and a couple of coffee dates?"

He leaned toward her. "I got all of that the moment I met you six months ago."

He held her gaze, the tension simmering between them. His plump lips glistened, probably from the wine, but it was the straw that broke the camel's back, so to speak.

Impulsively, she leaned forward, pressing her lips to his.

Finally.

The thought flitted through her brain as if some part of her had been waiting for this moment, this kiss, since they'd met. Maybe some part of her had been. After all, her rule against serious relationships had never kept her from enjoying the company of a man. But she'd run from Brandon after only a few dates. She'd known he was trouble and boy did it look like she was right. This one kiss alone had her feeling warm all over, and she was all too aware that there was a bedroom—given the size of this house, likely more than one—only a few steps away.

With a jerk, she broke off the kiss.

She grabbed her wine and finished off the glass in one gulp.

"Would you care for more wine?" Brandon asked, a knowing smile on his face.

"No. I'm fine, thanks." She pushed her plate away and forced herself to focus on the reason she was there. Tanya. "So listen, I'm sorry about kissing you."

He frowned. "I'm not."

"It's important we keep things professional between us, especially since this is not a department-sanctioned investigation. I don't want to muddy the waters any more than they already are."

Brandon's frown deepened. "If that's what you want." He poured more wine in his own glass and took a long swallow.

"It is. And it goes without saying that everything I'm about to share with you has to be kept confidential. If we develop evidence sufficient to show that Tanya didn't commit suicide, I'll have to decide on the best way to tell my lieutenant about your involvement in this case." Or whether to do so at all, but that was a problem for another day. "Until then, no one can know we are working together."

"Okay, I can live with those terms, but I have to be able to use my brothers." He held up a hand when she started to protest. "They don't have to be read in on the specifics of our alliance, but they have access to resources that neither you nor I do. It would be foolish not to use them. And as I've hired them as consultants on Tanya's case, they are bound by attorney-client privilege in addition to their usual promises of confidentiality. West Investigations is used to dealing with delicate situations. I have every confidence in them."

She didn't like it, but she didn't have much leverage. She wouldn't be able to tap into all the usual police sources since Wilson had ordered her to treat the case as a likely suicide, not if she wanted to keep her ongoing investigation from him. "Okay."

"Now." He smiled but it seemed more than a little forced. "I'm ready to hear all your secrets, Yara Thomas."

Chapter Ten

Yara pulled up the security video from Tanya's apartment on her phone, but the camera only caught a grainy shot of a man fitting the assailant's description entering and exiting the building through the garage. He'd kept his back to the camera as if he'd known they were there. The likelihood that his assailant had been Tanya's mystery man went up.

Yara caught him up on what she'd discovered about Tanya's case so far—the apartment paid for by a mystery man, the blood and fingerprints in the car and her lieutenant's determination that this was a suicide.

Brandon suggested they take advantage of the nice evening and continue their conversation on his patio. He grabbed what remained of the bottle of wine and their glasses and led Yara outside.

"Your garden is lovely," she said, settling into one of the four lounge chairs.

"Thank you. I find that gardening is a great stress reliever."

Her face registered surprise. "You did all this?"

She'd declined a second glass of wine earlier, but now she held out her glass for him to fill.

He filled her glass, then his own. "All by myself. It took a while. I made more than a few missteps, but I'm finally getting it to where I want it to be." He sipped.

"It's very relaxing." She let out a sigh.

"That's what I was going for."

"I shouldn't get too comfortable or you won't be able to get me out of here."

The last thing he wanted to do was get her out of his home. More like get her into the bedroom and out of her clothes. But he pushed that thought away.

"So, the case." She set her wineglass on the pavers next to the lounge chair and scooted to a semi-upright position. "You already know we found Tanya's body in her car on the stretch of Route 30. There's nothing around for more than a mile in either direction. Most of the traffic along that stretch sticks to the interstate."

"Which suggests Tanya was out there for a reason."

"Nothing was wrong with her car. We found the weapon that was used in the car on the console between the two front seats where it conceivably could have fallen if she'd shot herself."

"Yet, you didn't believe this was a suicide from the beginning."

She frowned. "I had my doubts. Mostly instinct if I'm honest. If Tanya wanted to kill herself, why drive out to some desolate road? If there's some significance to that spot, I don't see it. But what really gave me pause was her phone."

"Her phone?"

"Yes, so far we haven't found it or her computer."

A light bulb went off in his head. "Ah, that's why you asked me about her phone and phone number when we spoke earlier."

"Exactly. I don't know anyone without a phone nowadays and certainly not a twenty-nine-year-old. My partner suggested she might have left it back in her apartment so that no one could call her and talk her into changing her mind."

"But it wasn't there."

She shook her head. It was a warm night but there was a slight breeze blowing that had wrenched a tendril of hair from the knot at the base of her neck and now blew it across her face.

He scooted forward and tucked it behind her ear. He traced his thumb over her cheek, setting off a ripple of butterflies in his stomach. He was close enough to feel her body heat, smell the soft lilac scent of her perfume. His gaze dropped to her mouth and a buzz started low in his body. He leaned forward, but just before their lips would have met, she jerked back. The air between them chilled noticeably.

"Sorry," he said.

"No, it's fine." But he could tell it hadn't been. She seemed to be feeling the same attraction to him that he felt for her, but she was fighting it. Which made sense. She was a cop and he was an attorney. The flashing red light could not have been brighter. And yet he fought the urge to pick her up and carry her to his room. The impulse was almost overpowering. But she was giving off back-up vibes right and left, so he did.

"What were we talking about?" she asked.

"Tanya's missing phone."

"Right." She leaned back against her seat, putting more distance between them. "No phone and no computer."

"That is suspicious."

"Exactly. And the forensic tech found a small piece of cloth stuck to the back rear passenger side door, which admittedly is not much. But she also noted a gap in the blood spatter that made it into the back seat of the car."

"A gap?"

"Yes, as if something, or someone, had been sitting on the edge of the back seat leaning forward between the seats."

His heartbeat spiked. "Someone sitting like they might if they had a gun to the driver's head."

"Exactly. The only problem is the medical examiner says the angle of the shot is consistent with a self-inflicted wound and Tanya's are the only fingerprints we found on the gun."

"The killer could have worn gloves and wrapped her hand around the gun after he'd killed her. And couldn't someone get the same angle from the rear of the car if they were leaning forward?"

Yara stroked her chin with her hand. "I don't know. I'd have to ask."

"Okay, so that's something we need to nail down. West Investigations has all kinds of experts on staff.

I'll see if anyone there can answer the question generally. It won't hurt to have a second opinion. Anything else you think I should know?"

She shrugged. "That's all we've got. It's thin, but when you add it with the break-ins at Tanya's place, my instincts are telling me there's something there."

"I agree. We need to track down Tanya's boyfriend and the source of her unaccounted for income."

"I talked to one of Tanya's neighbors. But you know how it is in the city. Millions of strangers on your doorstep. She didn't remember ever seeing a man coming or going from Tanya's apartment. The doorman confirmed that she rarely had visitors, but we already know they could have come up through the garage without being seen."

"Why would a building where the residents pay out of the nose for the sense of security have such a glaring hole in security?"

"Because those same residents covet the privacy that glaring hole affords them so that they can do their dirty deeds without shame."

He exhaled heavily. "People don't make any sense."

"You are preaching to the choir." She swung her legs over the side of her chair and stood. "I should head home."

He pushed to his feet, too. "We didn't decide on our next steps."

"My next step is to head back to the Stryder Medical Clinic and hopefully catch Tanya's close friend and coworker. She hasn't returned my calls."

He walked with her to the door. "Were you thinking of dropping in on the coworker before or after work?"

Yara slid him a sidelong glance. "Why do you ask?"

They stopped at the door, but he didn't move to open it. "It would save time if I sat in on the interview with you. And if I just happen to be there at the same time, your boss couldn't fault you for that."

She fought back a smile. "Morning. I'm hoping to catch her before work."

He reached for the door, leaning in close. The air between them was charged. With his lips a breath away from her ear, he responded, "I'll bring the coffee."

Chapter Eleven

Brandon had just finished his morning workout in his basement gym when the doorbell rang. And rang again. And again. He didn't need to look out of the side window to know who he'd find standing on his front porch.

"Why are you ringing my bell like that?" He directed the question to Shawn, who still had his finger poised over the button. "And why are you letting him?" he asked. Ryan leaned against the railing.

"Because it annoys you," Shawn answered with a grin.

"And I let him because you didn't see fit to call and let anybody know you were attacked yesterday. By the way, James wants you to call him ASAP." Ryan shot a second devious grin his way.

Fantastic. All his brothers were going to gang up on him for failing to inform them he'd been jumped in a dead woman's apartment. Sometimes he longed to be an only child. "A call I look forward to." He stood back so his brothers didn't bowl over him as they stomped their way into his home.

He shut and locked the front door, then made his way to the kitchen. "Coffee?"

It was just shy of seven thirty and he'd planned to get an early start at the office before meeting Yara at the Snyder Medical Clinic, but he could tell his brothers had worked themselves into a lather. Hopefully, he could quickly assure them that he was fine and get his day back on track.

"So were you ever planning to tell us you got beat up?" Shawn grabbed the cup of instant coffee Brandon slid across the island countertop and sat on a stool.

"No. That piece of information didn't make it onto my to-do list, funny enough."

"You okay?" Ryan waved off the mug Brandon tried to hand to him.

"I'm fine." He looked from one brother to the next, letting them see that he wasn't trying to play a tough guy. The two ibuprofen he'd swallowed that morning had taken care of what remained of his headache. His cheek was still tender from the blow he took to the face, but the swelling was minimal.

Ryan scrutinized his face. His second-youngest brother was by far the most serious and focused of the four West brothers. It was why there hadn't been any argument when he assumed the helm of the family's security and investigations firm from their father when he retired. They'd all known Ryan was perfect to captain the family business. Shawn was the second-in-command, although technically he co-owned the firm with Ryan.

For his part, Brandon had never wanted to be a part of the family business beyond handling their legal affairs. He'd known early on that the law was his calling. A penchant for seeking justice and righting wrongs seemed to have been ingrained in him for as long as he could remember. He guessed it was ingrained in his brothers as well. James, the oldest West brother, had, until recently, made his career in the military, serving his country and protecting the freedom and rights of his fellow citizens. And both Shawn and Ryan had met the loves of their lives trying to save his now sisters-in-law from imminent danger.

"Okay, then why didn't you call and tell us what happened?" Shawn said, setting his coffee aside. He might have been the most laid-back brother, but when it came to family, he was as fiercely protective as any of the other Wests. "I had to hear about my own brother from a police contact."

"I'm sorry, but I knew if I told you two I'd never hear the end of getting my butt kicked."

"True." Shawn grinned.

Even Ryan let his lips turn up into a small smile. "Heard you called a detective on the Silver Hill force. Yara Thomas."

Shawn's brow formed a V and his forehead furrowed. "Thomas. I don't recall a Thomas on the detective squad."

"Pretty walnut eyes. Perpetual scowl. Severe bun," Ryan said.

"Oh, bunhead." Shawn snapped his finger. "Yeah, she's no fun at all."

"Don't call her that," he growled.

Brandon clutched the coffee mug in his hand.

Shawn's eyes widened and his grin grew twice as big. "You like her. No wonder you called her instead of one of us."

Brandon caught Ryan studying him out of the side of his eye. "She's the one you had a thing with last year, right?"

"It wasn't a thing."

"It was a thing. There were late-night calls. At least one date, if I remember correctly. You liked her. That's a thing."

Shawn pushed to his feet. "Hang on a minute." Indignation dripped from his voice. "You had a thing with bunhead and no one told me!"

Brandon stepped around the counter into his brother's personal space. "Don't. Call her. Bunhead."

Shawn put his hands up in surrender pose. "Okay, okay, sorry. You had a thing with Detective Thomas and Ryan knew and neither of you told me? Why?"

Brandon and Ryan answered at the same time.

"Because I can keep a secret."

"Because he can keep a secret."

"That's just messed up." Shawn sat back down on the stool.

"So?" Ryan said.

"So what?" Brandon grabbed the mug Ryan had waved away and took it to the sink, turning his back on his brothers.

There were only three years between him and Ryan and they were most alike of the four brothers. That engendered a natural camaraderie. It also meant they were able to read each other fairly well. He always knew when Ryan was holding back and Ryan had the same sixth sense when it came to him.

"She was the first woman you showed any serious interest in since your divorce and she stomped on your heart. So why'd you call her instead of one of us when you got your butt kicked?"

"She didn't stomp on my heart." Brandon turned to face his brothers, both of whom were looking at him with rapt attention. "And I called her because we're working on the case together."

"The one you had us looking into for you?" Ryan said.

"Yes."

"It's unusual for the cops to work with an attorney. Especially one who knows the victim and does mostly corporate work."

"I do pro bono work for a women's shelter, representing victims of domestic violence. That's actually what I initially thought Tanya Rutger had come to see me about, but now I'm not so sure."

"How does Detective Thomas figure into this?" Ryan pressed.

"She's the lead on Tanya's case."

Shawn hissed.

"Listen, I know," he said, coming back to stand at the island across from his brother. "But the medical examiner has issued a preliminary finding of suicide and I know Tanya wasn't suicidal."

"I take it the lovely detective feels similarly," Shawn responded.

"She has questions. But her lieutenant wants her to drop it so we've decided to work together off the books."

"Sounds like a plan that has disaster written all over it," Shawn quipped.

Ryan's brows arched. "For more than one reason."

"Look, whatever Yara and I had or might have had in the past, that is not what this is about."

"Dude, you were all in on her," Ryan countered.

Brandon threw up his hands. "We went out on two dates and exchanged exactly twelve phone calls. I wouldn't say that's all in."

"How many text messages?" Shawn deadpanned.

Ryan's laugh reverberated around the room.

Okay, so maybe he'd been enamored with Yara back then, but she'd made it clear she didn't want to see him romantically. Very clear. Like she'd gone radio silent. Stopped answering his calls, responding to his texts or returning his voice mails. He might have liked her but he could take a hint. She wasn't interested.

"You both need to go. I have to get ready for work." He shoved his brothers toward the front door.

"Okay, we're going. No need to paw at me. This is an Armani suit," Shawn said, dancing out of reach.

"Out. Now."

Shawn hopped off the porch and headed for the

sleek black BMW Brandon knew was part of the West fleet.

Ryan stopped in the doorway. "I just want you to be careful. With the case and with the detective. You can say what you want, but you've been hurt enough. That woman hurt you once. I don't want to see it happen again."

He knew Ryan's concern wasn't just about Yara. His divorce had been amicable as divorces go, but he hadn't wanted it. He believed in commitment and he'd wanted to try to fix his marriage. But Camille, his ex, had wanted out, so he'd let her go.

He laid a hand on Ryan's shoulder. Ryan was a man of few words, but he always made the ones he said count.

"I promise I'll be careful with the case and my heart."

He watched his brothers drive away and wondered if he'd be able to keep that promise.

Chapter Twelve

Yara parked in the lot designated for the Stryder Medical Clinic at exactly eight thirty the next morning. As was becoming a habit, her pulse quickened when she caught sight of Brandon getting out of his car with a to-go cup in each hand as she approached. Heavy clouds hung overhead, threatening rain, but Brandon wore only a navy sports coat over a white button-down and black slacks. He still looked like a million bucks.

"Good morning. I brought you a little something." He handed her one of the cups. "This coffee shop near my place makes the best cinnamon chai latte you will ever have. I guarantee it."

She took the cup but eyed it with suspicion. "I'm more of a regular coffee, cream and sugar kind of girl."

"No, no, no. Trust me on this." He held his own cup under his nose and inhaled deeply.

She had to admit, it smelled terrific. She took a sip. It tasted like heaven in a cup. "Not bad."

"See. I wouldn't lead you astray."

The look he gave her said just the opposite. That he'd love to lead her toward a host of decadently delightful acts. And she didn't need a mirror to glean that her expression said she was increasingly open to following him down that path.

Try as she had to keep things strictly professional between them, more and more of her day was being consumed with thoughts of kissing him. Not to mention her nights, when her thoughts went far beyond kissing.

A car door slamming had her shifting her gaze over Brandon's shoulder. "This looks like Bailey Dunlap." She set her cup on the hood of Brandon's car and headed toward the woman from the driver's license photo she'd pulled. "Bailey?"

The woman eyed her warily. "Yes?"

Yara flipped the cover on her badge open. "I'm Detective Thomas. I've been trying to reach you, Miss Dunlap. I have a few questions for you."

"Is this about Tanya?"

Bailey's gaze shifted from Yara to Brandon and back, questions in her eyes.

Brandon flashed a broad smile and Bailey visibly relaxed. "Brandon West." He extended a hand to Bailey and her body language shifted again from simply relaxed to receptive.

It appeared Brandon wasn't a bad guy to have around during female interviews.

That didn't stop the pang of jealousy that zipped through her.

"I understand you and Tanya were close," Yara said, pulling Bailey's attention from Brandon.

"We had become good friends in the months since she started working at Stryder Medical. I can't believe she's gone." Tears formed in the corners of Bailey's eyes.

Brandon pulled a white handkerchief from his inside blazer pocket. "I'm sorry for your loss."

Bailey took the handkerchief and dabbed at her eyes.

"I want to make sure the circumstances surrounding Tanya's death are thoroughly investigated," Yara said. "If you have a moment, I just have a few questions."

Bailey's face scrounged. "Circumstances? No one has told us much about how Tanya died."

"That's what we're working to find out. Do you know if Tanya had any problems with anyone recently?"

Bailey dabbed her eyes again, obscuring her face, but she shook her head. "She didn't mention anything."

"Any unhappy patients or a patient who showed too much interest in her?"

"No, nothing like that."

Bailey's gaze flicked back over to Brandon. He sent her another dazzling smile.

"I understand she recently broke up with her longtime boyfriend, Jasper Reinholt."

"I wouldn't say recently," Bailey said, shooting a glance at a passing car. "Tanya and Jasper broke up right after she started working for Stryder. I met him a couple of times and I don't think Jasper has a mean bone in his body. He certainly wouldn't hurt Tanya. He worshiped the ground she walked on."

"So the breakup wasn't his idea," Brandon said.

"Definitely not. Bailey initiated it. I know Jasper tried to talk her out of it."

"Was Jasper upset about the breakup?"

Bailey's expression clouded. "I don't want to get him in trouble. He's a good guy."

"Nobody is in trouble," Brandon slipped in smoothly. "We just need all the information we can get to put the pieces of Tanya's last days together. To get an accurate picture of what really happened to her."

Bailey hesitated for a moment longer. "Tanya said he tried to win her back. I think they went out to dinner once or twice after she'd called things off, but she wasn't really into it. She said the relationship had run its course."

"Do you know if they were in touch with each other recently?" Brandon asked.

Bailey hitched her purse higher on her shoulder and glanced at her watch. "I don't know. She didn't really talk about him much anymore."

The slight inflection on the word *him* made Yara wonder if there was someone else Tanya was talking to her friends about recently.

"Was there someone else in her life?"

Bailey glanced at the doors to the clinic and bit her bottom lip.

Brandon placed a hand on Bailey's shoulder. "Bailey, any information you give Detective Thomas will help her find out what happened to your friend."

"Okay, yeah. I want to help, but it's just, I'm not sure. Tanya was seeing someone, but she was really secretive about it. She said it was new, but I don't know. In the last couple weeks, though, she'd stopped mentioning her mystery man. That's what she called him, her mystery man."

That was little help. *Mystery man* wasn't a name she could run through the system. "She didn't tell you anything else that might help us identify him?"

Bailey shrugged. "I know he bought her a lot of presents. She was always coming to work with a new bag or new clothes when we'd go out."

"What about her apartment?"

Bailey frowned. "What about it?"

"Have you been?"

Bailey shifted from foot to foot. "A few times."

"Then you must have noticed it's very nice. Well beyond what a nurse would normally be able to afford. Not to mention the Mercedes."

"I did ask her about it, but she said she had some family money. I mean, we were friends, but she didn't show me her bank account."

"You said Tanya had stopped mentioning her mystery man in the last few weeks. Do you have any idea why?"

Bailey shrugged again. "No idea. She was all excited about this guy for months and then all of a sudden she wouldn't talk about him. I mean, it was pretty obvious what was going on. The guy must have been married. That never works out, you know." Something about the statement made Yara think Bailey was speaking from experience. "I figured the guy had moved on to the next woman or Tanya had gotten tired of being the sidepiece. I stopped asking when it was clear she didn't want to talk about it." She glanced toward the building again. "Look, I have to get to work."

Yara handed her a business card. "If there's anything else you remember, please give me a call."

Bailey gave her a tight smile but turned a brighter one on Brandon before walking away.

"Tanya lied about having family money," Yara said as she and Brandon headed back toward his car. "Her mother was a retired bus driver."

"Yeah, Mrs. Rutger didn't mention anything about family money to me when we spoke," he seconded. "But Bailey did confirm our mystery man theory."

Yara grabbed her now-cold latte from the top of Brandon's car and chucked it into the nearby garbage bin. "And it seems like the mystery man was on his way out. I wonder if that was his decision or Tanya's."

Brandon threw his coffee cup into the trash behind hers. "Well, we know that the breakup with Jasper Reinholt was her decision and that he wasn't happy about it."

She shot him a knowing look. "You think Jasper knows who the mystery man is?"

"If he suspected there was someone else, well, it would only be human nature to be curious."

She studied him out of the side of her eye. Had he wondered whether there was someone else when she'd cut off contact? Of course, there hadn't been. In fact, she hadn't been on a date since him. The feelings that had begun to build for him had scared her enough that she hadn't attempted dating again. But now, with Brandon back in her orbit and those feelings swelling again, a growing part of her was starting to regret giving in to her fear all those months ago.

Later. Right now they needed to speak to Jasper Reinholt.

"Okay, we don't know who Tanya's mystery man is, but we do know the ex-boyfriend's name and where he works. I say we speak to him next."

"Sounds like a smart plan. Not that I'd have expected any less from you."

She used her phone to google Jasper Reinholt. "It looks like Jasper's morning class lets out at noon. Want to meet me at Blair Hall on the Silver Hill Community College campus at eleven fifty?"

"I'll be there."

"Detectives."

They both turned to find a tall blond man in a black rain slicker and carrying a beat-up leather bag hurrying toward them.

Dr. Anand Gristedes. Yara and Martin had spoken to Tanya's bosses and the heads of the Stryder Medical Clinic, Dr. Gristedes and his partner, Dr. Steven Manning, after finding Tanya's body.

Dr. Gristedes swept an assessing gaze over Brandon before dismissing him.

Out of the corner of his eye, Yara saw Brandon's expression darken.

"Detective, has there been any progress? Do you know what happened to Tanya?"

"We're still investigating," Yara answered.

"Oh." Gristedes's face fell. "When I saw you talking to Bailey I thought there might be some news."

"Brandon West. Dr. Anand Gristedes. He's one of the partners in the Stryder Medical Clinic."

Yara made the introduction.

The two men shared a perfunctory handshake.

Male egos. Yara mentally shook her head. "Have you thought of anything else that might help us with the case?"

"No, I'm sorry. I told you everything I knew when you came to tell us about Tanya. I didn't really know her well. She'd been working with us for less than a year. It's just so unbelievable."

"If you do think of anything, don't hesitate to give me a call." She was anxious to get to the station. If she wanted this investigation to fly under Lieutenant Wilson's radar, getting to work late wasn't the way to do it.

Gristedes nodded and walked away.

"Doctors and their egos." Brandon huffed.

Yara walked backward toward her car. "You know, some would say the same about lawyers. I'm just saying." She laughed at his grumbling as she walked away.

BRANDON PARKED IN his designated space on the parking lot adjacent to his Silver Hill law offices and got out of the car still thinking about the interview with Bailey. The nurse had given them a place to start digging with Jasper Reinholt, but there was something about Dr. Anand Gristedes that he didn't like. Something that didn't involve his male ego, despite what Yara thought.

He headed for the entrance to the building.

"Hey! Ah… Mr. West."

Brandon turned to find Tanya's brother emerge from a black pickup truck and jog toward him.

"Mr. Rutger." Brandon held out his hand and Nick only hesitated slightly before he took it and shook. "What can I do for you?"

"Were you serious about looking into my sister's death?"

"I was. I am."

"Okay, then I want to help."

"Let's take this into my office."

Brandon led the younger man inside the building and into his office, asking his secretary to hold his calls.

Nick declined coffee and water and sat across from his desk. "The cops aren't going to investigate my sister's death. They've already decided she committed suicide."

Not all the cops, Brandon thought, settling into his own desk chair, but he didn't correct Nick. Yara was taking a chance continuing to look into Tanya's death and he wouldn't risk her career, not even to allay a grieving brother's concerns. Anyway, he was right about the department's overall take on Tanya's case.

"Well, I don't think she did and I'm going to do everything in my power to find out what really happened. You can help me by telling me everything you can about your sister. Anything could be of help."

Nick let out a heavy breath. "She'd pulled away from the family recently. Ever since she broke up with Jasper. At first, I just figured she needed time to cope with the breakup, you know. But I know my mother told you about the argument she and Tanya had. Not speaking to Ma like that, it just wasn't Tanya. I knew something else was up, but she wouldn't tell me what it was."

"What about her apartment? How did you think she was paying for it and the car?"

Nick scowled. "I didn't know about that. You have to understand, I'm seven years older than my sister. We weren't ever close. I loved her. I watched out for her, but we were always at different stages. I knew she'd moved downtown but mostly we exchanged texts checking in on each other and saw each other at Ma's house for holidays. I'd never been to her new place."

"But you knew Tanya was upset about something?"

"Yeah, just the way she lashed out at my mother. Ma only told me that they'd argued over Tanya's new boyfriend. When I reached out to Tanya, she went on about Ma nosing around in her personal life and how she was a grown woman and could date anyone she wanted. Our mother doesn't always respect boundaries so I kind of understood where Tanya was coming from and I just wanted to keep the peace between them. Ma didn't tell me she suspected Tanya was fooling around with a married man until after…" His voice broke.

Brandon gave him a moment to compose himself. "Do you have any idea who the man might be?"

"I really wish I did. If I knew, I'd confront the cheat myself," Nick growled. "You asked my mother about Tanya's cell phone and computer. Why?"

He had to tread carefully here. He only knew about the missing electronics because of his side investigation with Yara. "They seem to have gone missing."

"Missing? That's…weird. Tanya was attached to that phone. She always had it with her. And I know she had a laptop. A good one. I helped her pick it out. I work in IT."

Brandon pushed a legal pad and a pen across his desk. "Can you write down the type of computer and anything else about it that might make it identifiable as Tanya's? Same with the phone if you know what type she had."

Nick scribbled on the pad before handing it back over. "You think there might be something on them that could lead us to whoever killed her?"

"I don't know, but I don't like that they haven't been found."

"Wait, Tanya told me she'd started keeping a video diary. I thought it was kind of kooky. There might be something in it that would lead you to her new boyfriend." Nick stood. "I have to get to work, but I know what cloud service Tanya used. I can try to figure out her password and log in. Maybe she saved the diary there. It can't hurt to look, at least."

Brandon hesitated. "It might be best to let the police handle that. If you tell me the cloud storage provider, I'll pass it on to the detective on the case."

Nick shook his head. "No way. They had their chance. And this is something I can do for my sister."

He could tell he wouldn't be able to convince the man. Nick probably had the best chance of breaking into Tanya's cloud storage, certainly a better chance than he or Yara did, but he didn't want the man to do anything that might make him a target of whoever had killed Tanya.

"I think that would be okay, but you need to let me know right away if you are able to gain access."

"Agreed." Nick shook his hand and left.

Yara was not going to like having Nick dabble in the case, but it was something for Nick to do, something to help him through the grief.

And if they were lucky, he might even find evidence that pointed them to Tanya's mystery man.

Chapter Thirteen

The police station was abuzz with morning activity when Yara arrived at nine fifteen. It was unusual for her to get in later than the other detectives with whom she shared an office, but they were all at their desks when she slid into her chair. She knew that forensics had sent her a message about some prints they'd pulled from the last home robbery and she wanted to have a handle on the new developments in the case before Lieutenant Wilson inevitably asked her about it. She turned on her computer and waited impatiently for the screen to illuminate.

"So you finally made it in," Martin said and smiled.

She speared him a look over the top of her computer monitor. "I overslept." The login square popped up on screen and she quickly typed in her information.

Paris slid her chair over to Yara's desk. "You look pretty bright-eyed and bushy-tailed for a woman who overslept. Might there be a handsome reason for your sudden exhaustion?"

"My alarm didn't go off. I must have forgotten

to set it. That's the reason," she said, giving Paris a light push back toward her own desk.

Paris's face fell. "Oh, well, that's sad for you." She rubbed her rounded stomach and scooted back behind her desk.

Yara navigated to her emails and opened the one from the fingerprint lab. They'd found a match for one of the prints they'd pulled from the most recent house that had been burglarized. Zachary Brooks.

She pulled Brooks's record. A couple of pops for possession that were several years old and several arrests for assault, one of which got him an eighteen-month stint in jail. And a more serious charge for attempted murder that was subsequently dropped after the victim refused to testify and left the state. His prints on the dresser in Tanya's master bedroom suggested he might have graduated from assault to burglary. Brooks's record didn't list an employer but there was a note in the file that mentioned he sometimes did off-the-book work at a friend's landscaping company, Marymount Garden and Landscaping. It's the kind of work that would give a would-be burglar access to homes, but it wouldn't explain finding his fingerprints inside the house. Zachary Brooks was definitely looking like someone she needed to talk to.

"Thomas!"

She jumped at the sound of Wilson's voice. Turning in her chair, she found the lieutenant standing just inside the door to the bullpen. "Where have you been? I've been looking for you to get an update on those robbery cases."

She stood. "Sorry, sir. I got in a little later than usual today, but I was just about to come see you. We got a hit on a set of prints from the last burglary." She pointed to her screen and Wilson moved closer to get a look. "Zachary Brooks. He's got a record for assault. Got off on an attempted murder charge. He works under the table for a landscaper, so he might have had a reason to be at the subject house."

Wilson's eyes traced over the screen.

"I'm going to contact the homeowners. See if they use this landscaping company for their yard work and then have a chat with Zachary Brooks."

"Pick Brooks up. Do the interview here. You might rattle a confession out of him." His eyes found Martin. "Rachlin, you go with Thomas to arrest this guy. There are eyes on us. I don't want him slipping through our fingers."

She pressed her lips together tightly, smarting at the implication that she would let a potential arrestee get by her. It had never happened. It would never happen.

Wilson turned back to Yara. "Let me know when he's in the box." He strode away without another word.

She reclaimed her seat and reached for the phone.

A half hour later, Yara had confirmed with the homeowners and Marymount Garden and Landscaping that Zachary Brooks had done work at several of the residences that had been robbed, but that there was no reason his fingerprints should have been inside any of the homes.

The bright side was that maybe if she got the robberies tied up in a nice little bow for the lieutenant, he'd back off her some, giving her a little more wiggle room to investigate Tanya's case without feeling like she was under a microscope. The bad news was that she wouldn't be able to meet Brandon at Silver Hill Community College and speak with Jasper today.

She pulled her phone from her pocket and typed out a quick message.

SORRY. WORK STUFF. CAN'T MEET TODAY. WILL CALL LATER.

Twenty minutes later, Martin pulled the black Crown Victoria to a stop across the street from a run-down clapboard house where Zachary Brooks lived with his mother, Maxine. Gray and dingy, the remnants of snowfall from the prior week still edged the home's small yard. The rain that had been threatening while she and Brandon talked to Bailey came down as a light drizzle now, but the dark gray of the overhead clouds threatened showers on the horizon.

"What do we know about the mother?" Martin asked as they exited the car.

Yara pulled the hood of her jacket up, covering her head although she knew the moisture would find a way to twist her sleek ponytail into a mass of curls no matter what she did. "She's forty-two. An office administrator for a local trucking company for the past seventeen years and has no criminal record," Yara recited from the information she'd read in Zachary's criminal file. A file she'd sent to Martin while she finalized the warrant, but one he obviously hadn't read.

Frigid air stung Yara's cheeks as she stepped from the car.

Martin joined her on the sidewalk in front of the house.

Yara led the way up the cracked and crumbling walkway to the front door. She climbed the two steps of the small stoop and stood to the side of the door. Martin remained at the bottom of the stoop, flanking the other side of the door, the end of his coat hiked up so that he could reach his weapon.

Yara knocked on the door.

Seconds turned into a full minute and when no one responded, she knocked again.

The door finally swung open. She recognized Zachary's mother, Maxine, from her driver's license photo. Her face was a study in angles-jutted cheekbones and a sharp pointed nose. She wore her dark brown hair in an elaborate braided style. Her black skirt and stocking feet signified her recent arrival home from work.

Yara unclipped the badge she wore on her hip and held it out toward the woman. "I'm Detective Thomas and this is Detective Rachlin." She gestured behind her to Martin.

Maxine's dark eyes narrowed and her mouth

puckered before she schooled her face into a bland expression.

Yara's shoulders tensed. The rain began to beat down harder.

"We'd like to talk to your son, Zachary. Is he here?"

"No." Maxine blinked twice. She was lying.

Yara glanced over the woman's shoulder into the house but saw only an empty living room. "Can we come inside and look around?"

Maxine pulled the door closer to her body, cutting off even more of her view of the inside of the house. Her mouth puckered again. "Do you have a warrant?"

Yara sighed internally, but kept her tone professional. "We do not."

"Then you can't come in." Something, fear, maybe, flashed in Maxine's eyes. She flicked a quick glance to her right.

Years of reading witnesses' body language told her Zachary was inside, probably listening. Yara wouldn't have put it past Zachary to have threatened his own mother to keep her from speaking with the cops.

But if Maxine wouldn't consent to let them enter the house, they couldn't go in.

Yara persisted. "When was the last time Zachary was in your home, ma'am?"

"I don't have to answer your questions." The woman took a step backward, preparing to close the door.

Yara wedged her foot between the door and its frame. "No, you don't. But it may be better for your son if you do. We're just looking to ask Zachary some questions about an incident that took place in Green Village."

She didn't want to give away too much concerning the nature of the questions so Zachary wouldn't have time to think about how he might answer them.

Maxine's gaze flicked to the side once more and frowned. She wasn't going to talk.

Yara fished a business card out of her pocket. "If you see or hear from Zachary, please have him call me."

Maxine took the card and shut the door.

Yara stepped off the stoop and walked next to Martin back to the sedan, the crumbling walkway crunching under their boots.

"You do have a way with people," Martin said, his smile sardonic. They slid back into the car, Yara on the passenger's side, Martin behind the wheel.

Maxine peeked out from behind the living room curtain.

Frustration tightened in her chest. "Zachary's in there."

"Yep. And there's nothing we can do about it," Martin said, starting the car and cranking the dial for the heat.

A blast of cold air hit her in the face.

She hadn't been sure about Zachary's involvement in the robberies when she and Martin had pulled up to the house, but his reaction had boosted him to the top of the list of suspects. She didn't like being put off. And if she was wrong and he wasn't involved, she needed to know that and move on with the investigation. Chasing him down only to find out that he had a rock-solid alibi was a waste of time and resources that they didn't have.

Martin put the car in gear and pulled away from the curb.

Yara spotted the movement out of the corner of her eye. "Hang on. Look there." She pointed to a shadow along the side of the house.

Someone crept toward the front corner of the house. The outdoor light mounted to the neighbor's eave cut through the grayness of the day enough that she recognized the figure as Zachary.

Zachary surveyed the street, his eyes landing on Yara's through the windshield. He pivoted on his heels and ran into the shadows between the two houses.

Martin hit the sirens. "He should have at least waited until we drove away."

Yara grabbed the large Maglite from the glove compartment and reached for the door handle. "I'll follow on foot."

Martin would call for backup and circle the block in the car. Wilson's comments about eyes being on the department concerning these robberies rang in Yara's head. If Zachary got away, he could go to ground and it might be weeks before they located him again.

A narrow alley ran between the backyards of the houses fronting parallel streets. Unfortunately, many of the yards had fences and gave Zachary several places to lay in ambush. The robberies hadn't involved any violence to date, but that didn't mean Zachary didn't have a weapon.

Yara put her back against the nearest fence and drew her weapon. Taking a deep breath, she rounded the fence gun first. Her heart hammered so loud she was sure it would give away her location. She could feel sweat seeping through her undershirt.

She huffed breaths as she scanned the surrounding yards for her suspect.

Why did people leave so much stuff out in their yards? Doghouses. Sheds. A big decorative rock. What was the point?

Martin had killed the siren, but Yara saw the blue and red strobe lights at the end of the alley just before the hood of the Crown Vic became visible. Martin swept the tactical light mounted on the side of the car over the alley, illuminating the space.

Something moved at the opposite end of the alley. Zachary had made it farther down the alley than she'd expected. But the light must have scared him. He darted from behind a toolshed, through a yard, and ran hard toward the street adjacent to his mother's house.

"Police. Stop," she yelled, knowing it would do no good. She pounded behind Zachary.

The alleyway was really nothing more than a cut-through, too narrow for the Crown Vic to fit, but Yara heard the peel of tires as Martin raced along the side street.

The foot chase had attracted the attention of several neighbors. Outdoor lights flashed on, helpfully illuminating Zachary in the now nearly torrential rain, sprinting some thirty yards ahead of her. Unfortunately, some of the neighbors had decided to get themselves a front-row seat to the action. Doors were opening, curious faces peeking out.

"Go back inside and lock your doors now!" Yara yelled. If Zachary got tired of running and he did have a gun, he could very well decide that his best way out of the situation was to open fire.

She dug deep and forced her legs to move faster. She heard the Crown Vic's engine roaring down the street behind her and caught the swirl of the car's lights as Martin sped past her. Yara anticipated Martin's goal—cutting Zachary off at the end of the block.

Unfortunately, so had Zachary. He cut across the street, so close to the Crown Vic's bumper that she flinched in anticipation of Zachary's body hitting the hood of the car.

Somehow Zachary made it to the other side of the street without getting struck and darted behind yet another house.

What was he doing robbing houses? The guy could have been a track star.

She cut across the yards, slowing now that she didn't have the neighbors' front porch lights to help her make out shapes through the rain. She fanned the Maglite back and forth. She could hear more sirens in the distance. Backup was on the way.

A dog barked to her right and a chain-link fence rattled.

She swung the flashlight in that direction and caught sight of Zachary going over a fence two yards away.

"Police. Get on the ground now."

Just as before, he kept moving.

She ran for the fence Zachary had just gone over, holstering her gun to jump the fence and pulling it out again almost the moment her feet hit the ground. That Zachary hadn't tried to ambush her was a good sign that he didn't have a weapon, but she wasn't taking any chances. She ran through two more yards and over a gravel-strewn driveway, the rocks pummeling her shins as she ran.

The sirens were louder now but Yara didn't see any black-and-whites. She chased Zachary into another narrow alleyway, spying him twenty feet ahead. Maybe Zachary would have been a better sprinter than a long-distance runner. He'd noticeably slowed. Lucky for her, she had run cross-country in both high school and college and had kept up with the sport for exercise.

Yara pumped her legs, opening up her stride and closing the distance between them. She lunged, propelling herself onto Zachary's back and taking them both to the ground. Her left knee slammed into a brick paver, sending pain shooting up and down her leg, but she didn't loosen her grip on Zachary.

Zachary lay beneath her, stunned and out of breath.

She recovered first. She dragged one of Zachary's arms behind his back, snapping a cuff on it as heavy footsteps raced around the corner of the house. Flashlights lit up the patio.

"I got him," Yara said, snapping the cuffs on Zachary's other hand.

The two uniformed officers took over as she pushed to her feet, still breathing hard, as Martin rounded the corner. "You okay?"

They watched the officers pick Zachary off the ground and read him his rights. He shot a look over his shoulder as they led him away that was pure menace.

Yara rubbed her knee. "I'm good. If you'd ever join me on my morning run you could have been right there beside me for all the action."

Martin slid his glasses from his face and gave each lens a swipe. "Naw. I'm too old for all that nonsense." He slipped his glasses back on his face. His eyes narrowed on the hand she was using to massage her knee. "I thought you said you were fine. You need to have that leg looked at."

Yara shook her head, limping toward the front of the house. "It's fine. Just bumped it against the ground. We need to get back to the station and question Zachary."

"I guess he definitely knows something about the robberies," Martin said.

Patrol cars littered what she suspected was usually a quiet street. The red and blue strobe lights had attracted a crowd despite her order to the neighbors to remain inside. Half a dozen people stood on their front stoops or in the front yards of their homes enjoying the show.

"Looks that way." Yara watched the patrol car with

Zachary in the back seat maneuver around the Crown Vic, which Martin had left parked catty-corner to the sidewalk. "Lieutenant Wilson will be happy."

Chapter Fourteen

Brandon was disappointed to get Yara's text canceling their noon rendezvous with Professor Jasper Reinholt. After a brief period of consideration, he decided to speak to Jasper on his own. The attack on him at Tanya's apartment had made the situation more than just a quest to do right by his client. It had made the situation personal.

So Brandon was waiting in the corridor of Blair Hall at noon when students began streaming out of the classroom where Jasper had just finished teaching Anthropology 201: Ecological and Evolutionary Anthropology. He waited for the students to clear the door, then went inside.

Jasper Reinholt stood at the lectern at the front of the class stuffing papers into a backpack. He was about five foot six, thin with dark, almost black, hair and square rimless glasses. He wore dark brown corduroy pants and a brown-and-white-checked shirt with his sleeves rolled up to his elbows. There were no scratch marks or bruises on his hands or the parts of his arms that were visible, and Jasper was at least forty pounds and three inches too small to be the man who had attacked him at Tanya's place.

That didn't mean he wasn't her killer, though.

"Professor Reinholt?"

Jasper looked up from collecting his things. "Yes?"

"My name is Brandon West." He plucked a business card from the gold-plated holder in the breast pocket of his blazer and handed it over. "I was retained by Tanya Rutger prior to her death."

Jasper's eyes widened. "Retained for what?"

"I can't get into that, I'm sorry." Literally couldn't get into it, but Jasper didn't need to know that. "I'm hoping you can answer a few questions and help me sort a few things out. I understand you and Tanya dated for a period. I'm sorry for your loss."

"Thank you, that's kind of you to say. But Tanya and I have been broken up for some time now."

"I did hear that you'd broken up. When was the last time you saw Ms. Rutger?"

Jasper played with the business card in his hand. The man was nervous. But that wasn't altogether unusual. Having an attorney show up at your workplace and start asking questions about your dead ex-girlfriend had the tendency to make some people nervous.

"We broke up six months ago."

Brandon noted that Jasper hadn't answered the question, but he was willing to give the man a little bit of rope. "So you hadn't seen or spoken to Tanya in six months?"

Jasper glanced around the empty classroom nervously.

He already knew the answer to the question based on what Bailey had told him and Yara earlier that morning, but he could see Jasper trying to work out whether to tell the truth or to lie.

"I saw her a few times after the breakup. Why are you asking me all these questions?"

He injected warmth into his smile, knowing it would have the effect of calming the jittery man. "As I said, Tanya hired me, and although she is unfortunately no longer here, I want to complete the job I was hired to do." Not an untrue statement even if he didn't know what the job he was hired to do was. "The few times you saw Tanya after your breakup, when was that?"

"I don't know for sure. We broke things off in early March and I think it was a few weeks after that, so late March, early April."

"And what did you do?"

Jasper's expression relayed confusion. "What do you mean?"

"When you met. Did you go out to dinner? Catch a movie? Hit a bar?"

"Oh, ah, well one time we did go out to dinner and a movie. Another time I think we just stayed in and watched something on the television."

"So the breakup was amicable? You remained friends?"

"Yeah, I mean, I guess."

Brandon pressed. "You guess?"

Jasper let out a heavy sigh. "Look, I mean it was amicable as far as breakups go. I didn't want the relationship to end. Tanya did. I thought maybe if I paid her more attention, you know, she'd come back to me, so I convinced her to let me take her to a nice dinner and let me come over to watch a movie. But like, her mind was made up. Said we could stay friends. Well, I don't drop two hundred dollars on dinner for my friends so eventually I just let her go."

"When you two met up at her place to watch a movie, was that her place in Lower Manhattan?"

"No. She was still living in the apartment in Queens when we were together."

Brandon studied the man with a practiced eye. "But you knew about the new apartment in Lower Manhattan?"

Jasper nodded. "Yeah, I knew."

"Did you wonder where she got the money for a place like that?"

"Of course I did. The money for rent and the money for the car."

"And did you do some amateur investigating and find out?"

Jasper smirked. "Okay, I tried. You would have, too. We'd been dating for nearly two years. I was thinking about asking Tanya to be my wife. Then out of the blue she dumped me and is living large in a fancy apartment. Driving a luxury car. So I was curious, but I never found out how she was paying for it. Or who was paying for it for her."

"But you think someone was paying for her new lifestyle for her."

"Well, I mean, yeah. I know how much she made and it wasn't enough to cover that apartment and car. Her mother's pension barely covers her expenses and her brother can't keep a job, so it's pretty clear where the money is coming from."

"And where do you think that was?"

"A new man. Tanya always had big dreams. She loved helping people, don't get me wrong, but she also wanted nice things. Like, really nice things that she could never have afforded on a nurse's salary. She must have found some guy who was willing to foot her bills and she traded up. I thought maybe…"

"You thought maybe what?"

"We were just fine before she got that job with those two doctors. I had a feeling the new guy might work there or at the hospital that the clinic is affiliated with."

Jasper looked away but Brandon didn't miss the hurt on the man's face. He felt bad for him. It appeared that Jasper really had cared for Tanya. Which didn't mean he was innocent. The majority of people murdered die at the hands of someone who professed to love them.

"Did you ever confirm that feeling?"

Jasper sighed again. "Look, I admit I poked around on Tanya's social media pages, asked a few mutual friends if they'd heard about a new guy, but I turned up nothing, and at the end of the day I'm not the kind of guy who doesn't take no for an answer. I moved on."

Brandon believed him. Nothing in Jasper's tone or body language indicated he was being deceptive. And his reaction to being unceremoniously dumped then seeing his ex's lifestyle dramatically change wasn't unreasonable.

"Have you ever driven on Route 30 north?"

Jasper started at the sudden change in topic, but recovered quickly. "Ah, yeah. A bunch of times. I've taken that road to avoid traffic on the interstate. Why?"

"Just curious."

Jasper swallowed hard, making his Adam's apple bob. "I heard Tanya was found in her car on a road somewhere. Is that where...?"

"Yes, along Route 30. Do you have any idea why she would have been out there?"

Jasper shook his head, sending a dark curl falling into his face. He pushed it back into place absently. "No. I mean, Tanya did go with me to have Thanksgiving dinner at my aunt and uncle's place last year, but I can't imagine her going to visit them on her own. Why would she?"

That did seem to be a long shot, but maybe she'd met her new boyfriend while she and Jasper were at Thanksgiving dinner. "Was there anyone at that Thanksgiving other than you, Tanya and your aunt and uncle?"

Jasper shook his head. "Just the four of us."

That didn't mean Tanya hadn't met her mystery man at that time, although it made it less likely. But it meant she knew about the lightly traveled road. Maybe she'd planned to meet someone out there and something had gone wrong. It was a link between Tanya and the place her body had been found, however tenuous. Maybe if he and Yara pulled at the threads a little more they'd find something.

Jasper hooked his backpack over his shoulder. "Is there anything else? It's my lunchtime and I have another class in an hour."

"No. Thank you for speaking to me."

Jasper took several steps toward the door, then turned back. "Tanya and I might not have been together anymore, but I still cared about her. She didn't deserve that. I hope whatever it is you're doing for her, it helps find her killer."

He hoped so, too.

Chapter Fifteen

Zachary's cold eyes locked on Yara as she entered the interrogation room. He sneered but remained silent.

Yara settled into the chair across the table from him.

"How are you doing, Zach?" She tossed a legal pad and opened the file she'd carried into the room. Zachary's rap sheet. He'd had his first encounter with the law at the ripe old age of eleven, picked up for selling weed. His initial contacts with the system had all been with the juvenile courts. But as he'd gotten older, his criminal offenses had become increasingly more serious.

Zachary had completed three years of a seven-year sentence for the grand larceny for stealing several automobiles as part of a car theft ring. He'd been released on parole last September and, from the looks of things, had taken up right where he'd left off. The detectives in the gang unit suspected he was involved in the robberies of several drug dealers since he'd been released from prison. Unfortunately, his stint in prison seemed to have made Zachary a better criminal than when he'd gone in and they hadn't been able to develop enough evidence for an arrest.

"So, Zach," she said. "Why'd you run from me?"

"I ain't got nothing to say to you." He leaned back in the chair in a position that was designed to convey nonchalance.

Zachary was a dangerous criminal, but his round face and sun-kissed blond hair gave him an air of undeserved innocence. In a Ralph Lauren T-shirt, designer jeans and three-hundred-dollar sneakers, he could have passed for a rich college student home for a visit.

Yara nodded. "True. You don't have to talk to me, but I bet if we looked really hard, we could find something for your PO to violate you on. You know these parole officers. Sticklers for the rules. How many years do you have left on your sentence?"

He glared.

"Four years," she answered her own question. "Four years all because you went all Usain Bolt on me."

He shifted in his seat, stretching his legs out in front of him, one of which was chained to a metal hook in the floor. He crossed his legs at the ankle and his arms across his chest.

She mimicked the pose, sending a saccharine smile across the table as he did. "Maybe you wanted to go back so you could spend more time with Aiden."

Zach drew his body ramrod straight. "You keep my brother's name out of your mouth."

It looked like the sibling connection was the right

button to push. Aiden Brooks had taken after his brother and was currently serving a seven-year sentence for assault.

"Two peas in a pod. Or two criminals in the clink, as the case may be," she said as if he hadn't spoken.

His eyes flashed something cold and threatening.

She straightened but kept his smile fixed on his face.

Someone knocked on the door and a split second later Lieutenant Wilson stuck his head inside the room. "Detective, can I speak to you for a moment?"

Annoyance tripped in Yara's stomach. She was just getting started with her interrogation, setting the rhythm, getting Zachary wound up. Stepping out of the room now meant he'd have time to recalibrate and she'd have to start all over again, but she really didn't have a choice.

She stepped from the interview room, surprised to find Lieutenant Wilson and Morgan Corbett, assistant district attorney, and another man. "What's going on?"

"Detective Thomas, you know ADA Corbett and this is Jung Hsiung, an investigator with the ADA's office."

She nodded an acknowledgment at each of the men. "Okay. Why are they here?"

"We're taking custody of Zachary Brooks," Morgan said, the slight upward quirk of his mouth letting her know he was enjoying stealing her suspect out from under her.

Two years ago, she'd reluctantly agreed to go out

with Morgan on what had turned out to be the date that would not end. He'd taken her to one of the many chic New York restaurants where diners paid a fortune for a meal that wouldn't fill up a hummingbird. Morgan had spent the entire meal talking about himself—his Ivy League undergraduate and law degree, being one of the youngest attorneys in his division, his goals of one day assuming a judgeship. By the time the check had come, she was more than ready to head home. As was Morgan, only the home he'd wanted to head to was hers and he seemed to think she should feel honored that he wanted to spend the night. She'd made it clear in no uncertain terms that he was not invited up, which had not gone over well. Their professional relationship had been frosty ever since and she'd done her best to keep her distance.

She fisted her hands on her hips. "He's being charged with multiple counts of burglary. You can't just come in here and take custody."

"Our case trumps a few home invasions," Morgan said. "You can have him back when we're done with him."

"What's your case?" Yara spat.

Morgan shook his head. "Sorry. Can't tell you that. It's a need-to-know and you don't need to know right now."

"You're taking my suspect, but you can't tell me why?"

"Exactly. All you need to know is that Zachary Brooks is a material witness in a very important and sensitive case."

"A material witness in what case?"

She glanced at Lieutenant Wilson, but for all his bluster about the mayor's interest in the case, he was conspicuously quiet now. "And when will that be?" she asked.

Morgan shrugged. "Don't know. Depends on how much he can tell us and how long the case takes to prosecute."

He gestured toward the interview room and his investigator stepped forward and opened the door.

She and Lieutenant Wilson watched from the hall as Morgan and the investigator explained to Zachary why they were there and that he was now in their custody.

Zachary didn't look surprised by Morgan's sudden appearance, which only stoked the ire Yara felt. It appeared that everyone but her knew what was going on. And she didn't like being on the outside one bit.

BRANDON OPENED THE door as Yara started up the walkway. The zing of excitement he'd felt upon seeing her car pull to a stop in front of his townhome was quickly replaced by throbbing anger. She limped to the door and up close now, he could see that her bottom lip was split.

"Are you okay? What happened?" He reached a hand out to help her into the house. Her hair fell in tousled waves and made him think about all the ways he'd love to tousle it even more.

But she was in no state for those kinds of thoughts, so he forced himself to ignore the tightening in his groin. Closing the door with his foot, he then wrapped an arm around her waist, prepared to lift her in his arms and carry her to the living room sofa.

She stopped him with a glare. "Don't you dare. I'm not an invalid. I can walk."

He bit his tongue and kept his arm firmly around her waist as she hobbled to his sofa. "What happened?" he asked again, moving to the kitchen to grab a bag of frozen peas from the freezer.

"Foot chase. I banged my knee up a bit. Split my lip when I tackled the guy. I'm fine. I've taken harder hits from my brothers growing up."

"Someone needs to talk to your brothers about how to treat a lady, then," he muttered. "Here, lie back and put your leg up on the couch." He moved a couple of pillows so that she could prop herself up on the arm of the sofa and extend her leg, then laid the bag of peas over her knee.

She probably should have gone straight home to rest, but it secretly thrilled him that she'd chosen to come to him. He liked taking care of her, which would have probably been as much a surprise to her as it was to him if he told her, which he was absolutely not planning to do.

"I doubt my brothers thought of me as a lady, at least not when we were young. I'm fine. Physically at least."

He eyed her. "What does that mean?"

"I'm not hurt, not really, but I am angry. I get banged up chasing down the bad guy and Morgan Corbett swoops in and takes custody of him. And he won't even tell us why."

"Morgan Corbett, the assistant district attorney?"

"Yeah, you know him?"

"We went to law school together."

"Well, your old law school chum is a real piece of work. He said my suspect was a material witness in one of his cases but he wouldn't give any more details. So weeks of work and a bruised knee and I have nothing to show for it."

He moved back to the kitchen and grabbed two beers from the fridge, twisting the top off both bottles before returning to the living room. He sat on the coffee table across from her and handed her one of the bottles.

He tapped his bottle to hers.

They both took long sips.

"You know, Morgan and I keep in touch. I could give him a call. See if he'll share more details on his case with an old law school friend than with the cops."

Her hand stopped as she was lifting her beer to take another sip. "You would do that for me?"

He gazed at her. "That's the least of what I would do for you."

A blush bloomed on her cheeks. "Thank you. And sorry I had to cancel on you earlier."

He enjoyed the renewed sexual awareness between them but he sensed that she wasn't as comfortable with it, so he let her keep the conversation on steadier ground. "Not a problem." He knocked back another gulp of beer. "I actually decided to go see Jasper by myself."

"What? I thought we agreed you'd keep me in the loop."

"We did. Which is why I'm telling you now that I went to see Tanya's ex."

She pushed herself up straighter on the sofa. He could tell the movement had hurt even though she did her best not to show it. "That's not what I meant by keep me in the loop. I meant let me know what you are planning to do before you do it."

Rage at the man who'd hurt her threatened to rear up but he tamped it down.

"I didn't agree to that." He raised a hand before she could start in on him again. "Would you like to know what the professor said or would you rather keep yelling at me?"

She shot him a look that should have made him run for the hills, but somehow he found it endearing. God, she was even more gorgeous angry.

"What did he say?" she bit out.

He relayed the high points of his conversation with Jasper. She took everything in, only stopping him twice to ask clarifying points.

"So Jasper suspected Tanya's new man might be one of the doctors she'd come in contact with at the job. It's not a bad theory given all the money she seemed to have come into after starting that job."

"It's possible, but doctors don't necessarily have the disposable income that people think. Much like lawyers, the cost of the credential eats into your salary significantly and for a number of years."

"Okay, okay. I'm not going to be an elitist on doctors, but it's a theory that is worth looking into."

"I agree. I've started researching the practice, but there are seven doctors who work in the clinic and it is affiliated with a nearby private hospital so it's possible Tanya could have met someone through the clinic who works at the hospital."

Yara sighed. "Our suspect list is going in the wrong direction. Growing instead of shrinking."

"I know. That's why I've asked my brother to help by checking backgrounds. I figured it made the most sense to start with the clinic doctors and work our way outward."

"Agreed."

"I'm also not sure if there's any significance to be placed on the fact that Jasper and Tanya traveled along the road where Tanya's body was found."

Lines formed on Yara's forehead. "I don't know, either." She shifted on the sofa, then winced.

"Here, let me…" He grabbed the pillow from the other end of the sofa and moved to put it under the injured knee.

"No, it's okay. I should be going." She swung her leg over the side of the sofa and to the floor slowly.

He tossed the pillow aside and sat next to her. "You could stay. I have a guest room. Two, actually. You can have your pick."

Or she could stay in his bedroom. In his bed. In his arms. But something told him saying those thoughts out loud would send her running as fast as her bum knee would allow.

The corner of her mouth curved in a hint of a smile. "Thanks, but I can make it home."

He hooked his arm around hers and helped her to her feet.

Her knee threatened to buckle and he steadied her, pulling her in close. Closer than he had to, admittedly.

She looked up into his eyes, her dark brown ones softening, and filling his chest with a need he'd never felt before.

She surprised him by sliding her arms around his neck, going up on her toes and kissing him. Softly at first, but when he slid his arms around her waist, she deepened the kiss. He wanted to take it easy since she'd been hurt, but when he tried to back away, she held him firmly in place.

Her mouth was intoxicating. She nibbled at his bottom lip, an action that was so erotic his knees threatened to give way.

Finally, she pulled her mouth away from his, but remained in the circle of his arms. "Sorry, I don't know what came over me."

"You wound me. I'm not sorry at all. I think we've been building toward this from the first moment we met in the courthouse."

"Maybe." Her eyes swept over his mouth and he pulled her in closer.

"Why did you drop out of my life all those months ago? What did I do wrong?"

She swept a hand over his shoulder. "You didn't do anything wrong."

"Then why'd you walk away from me?"

"My job is dangerous. Every day I leave for work not knowing if I'll make it back home."

Brandon pushed a lock of hair behind her ear. "I've got news for you, Yara. No one knows if they'll make it until the end of the day."

Her eyes locked on his face. "You know what I mean. I never want to put you or anyone through the agony of having to pick up the pieces and go on if something happens to me on the job."

He held her tighter. "What about the agony of never knowing what we could have been because we never tried?"

The internal struggle between her fears and the possibility he'd put before her played out in the expression on her face.

He dropped a light kiss on her lips. "Just…think about what I said, okay?"

She pushed away, taking several steps backward this time.

"Okay," she said again. "But I really should go now."

He set aside his pent-up need. All things in good time.

He helped her to the door, holding it open for her. "You sure you can make it home on your own?"

"I'm sure. Good night, Brandon."

"Sweet dreams, Yara."

Chapter Sixteen

Brandon wasn't surprised that Morgan kept him waiting for nearly twenty minutes. He was surprised that his friend had agreed to see him on such short notice.

He sat on the comfortable leather sofa and went through his ever-growing email messages on his phone. At last a willowy young woman in a black skirt suit strode through the doors separating the offices from the reception area and asked him to follow her.

They walked down a brightly lit corridor lined with offices with glass front walls, her heels clicking on the tile floors. Brandon stayed close behind. It was clear from the day he'd started at the district attorney's office that Morgan was destined to be a rock star and it seemed that he was well on his way. His wasn't quite a corner office but it was definitely corner adjacent. The walls were lined with dark paneled bookshelves and leather-bound books Brandon would have bet good money Morgan had never cracked open. Through the office's glass wall, Brandon could see the man sat at an antique desk he'd had to have brought in himself—no way the government footed the bill for its cost—but Brandon couldn't deny the setup was impressive.

His escort knocked on the door.

Morgan raised his head and waved at them to enter. He stood as Brandon crossed the expansive office to shake his hand. "Brandon West, what a surprise. How long has it been?"

"It's been a while. Thank you for seeing me on short notice."

"Would you like something to drink? Water? Coffee?"

"Nothing, thanks."

"That will be all, Coleen." Morgan nodded at the woman who'd escorted Brandon to the office.

They both sat, Morgan in the leather executive chair behind his desk and Brandon in the silk upholstered chair in front of the desk.

It had been more than ten years since Brandon left the prosecutor's office, but Morgan looked as if he aged ten years in that time. Litigation work could do that to a person. Morgan had never been good-looking—his face was flat, and his eyes just a little bit too widely set. Now he looked frail, white dress shirt loose around the neck despite being buttoned up to the last button.

"I must admit, I'm curious as to why you reached out."

"It's about one of your cases. One that appears to have a connection to a client I represent."

"Oh?" Morgan leaned forward and placed his elbows on the desk, steepling his hands.

"You took a man into custody yesterday. Zachary Brooks. Yet, no one seems to know why."

Morgan's face darkened. "How do you know that?"

Brandon smiled. "We all have our sources and connections."

"That's confidential information."

"I heard he was a material witness in one of your investigations." He was taking a chance revealing this information, but a small one he figured. Morgan might suspect Yara had told him and that he was here on her behalf, but there wasn't much he could do about it beyond complain to her lieutenant. Yara was a big girl. She could handle a dressing-down if it came to that. She might not even mind if he got useful information here.

"I can't talk about my case."

"Not even to a former colleague?"

"*Former* being the operative word in that sentence."

"Come on, Morgan. Help me out here. You know I'm not going to share what you tell me with anyone."

"Why are you asking?"

He'd anticipated this question. He couldn't come out and tell Morgan that he was doing it for Yara, so he'd come up with another plausible excuse. "It may or may not have some bearing on a client of mine."

Morgan's right eyebrow rose. "One of the domestic violence cases you work on?"

Brandon let the silence do the work for him.

Morgan sighed. "This doesn't leave this room, got it?"

"Got it."

"Zachary Brooks is a material witness in a Medicare fraud and illegal sale of prescriptions case I'm working on."

Brandon wasn't sure what he was expecting, but it wasn't that. "How in the world did someone like Zachary get mixed up in Medicare and prescription fraud?"

Morgan chuckled mirthlessly. "These guys are like the Warren Buffett of crime. They're diversified to mitigate risks. Zachary's brother is serving seven years for an assault. Zachary came to us with information on the fraud in an effort to shave time off his brother's sentence."

"How did Brooks even know about the fraud?"

"His ex-girlfriend works at the practice that's the subject of our investigation. He overheard her talking about the fraud and got the bright idea to capitalize on it."

Brandon's senses tingled. "What's the girlfriend's name?"

"Bailey Dunlap."

PARIS DROPPED A file folder on Yara's desk the next morning as she waddled past.

"What is this?" Yara asked.

"Tanya Rutger's phone records."

Finally. Hopefully, there was something in them that would give her a name for Tanya's mystery man and explain why she'd been out on Route 30 the night she was killed.

The request for Tanya's phone records covered the thirty days prior to her death and included phone calls and texts. The text messages alone spanned nearly thirty pages. Yara flipped to the list of phone calls, relieved to find that it was a much more manageable ten pages.

She scrolled to the end of the phone list, working backward from the last call made. In addition to the number of the incoming or outgoing call, the records listed the date and time of each call, the city the call originated from and the duration of the call. Unfortunately, it didn't tell her the name of the listed owner of the other phone. She'd have to run each of the numbers through the reverse phone directory database and see if they got a hit, and that would take time.

Most of the calls were incoming. She was able to quickly identify and eliminate calls from Tanya's mother and brother. What really interested her were the nearly three dozen calls from a number that came up as the main line for the Stryder Clinic. There were any number of reasons that an employee might receive or make a phone call to their employer, but these calls mostly seemed to come at the end of the workday or well after the clinic would have been closed for the day. And there were far more calls from the clinic number to Tanya's phone than there were calls from Tanya to the clinic. In fact, when she broke the calls out into those that were sent and those that were received, she could see a definite pattern.

All the calls that Tanya had made to the clinic occurred during normal work hours. With the exception of two, all the calls that came from the clinic had come after the clinic should have been closed. There might have been nothing to it—maybe someone at the clinic had been calling to follow up on a patient or ask Tanya to come in for extra shifts, a lot of extra shifts—but Yara's instincts told her otherwise.

Unfortunately, there was no way to tell from the phone records alone exactly who'd been calling Tanya. Which meant another trip to the clinic was in order.

The only other number that had called Tanya's phone with any regularity was unlisted to Yara. But the name that popped up when she ran it through the reverse directory was not.

Jasper Reinholt.

Hadn't he told Brandon that he hadn't spoken to Tanya since giving up on winning her back? Yet there were four calls ranging from approximately five minutes to nearly forty minutes listed on Tanya's phone records well after their breakup. One of which had occurred the day before Tanya's body was found.

She flipped to the pages showing the text messages Tanya sent or received over the last month. There were nearly a dozen text messages from Reinholt's number as well. Many of them were mildly to openly flirtatious. None were threatening, but it wouldn't have been the first time someone went from love to hate faster than a speeding bullet. Maybe Tanya had tried to get rid of Jasper once and for all on one of the calls and he hadn't taken it so well. She'd had Reinholt far down on her list of people of interest given the consensus that his relationship with Tanya had ended several months earlier, but now he was someone she wanted to speak to sooner rather than later.

She reached for her cell phone and dialed another number that was becoming more and more familiar to her.

Brandon picked up after the first ring. "Detective, I was just about to call you."

She ignored the flip-flop in her stomach at the sound of his voice. "Didn't Jasper Reinholt tell you that he hadn't spoken to or seen Tanya in a few months?"

"Ah, well, then, right to business are we? Yes, that's what he told me. Six months, to be exact."

She lowered her voice to little more than a whisper. "I got Tanya's phone records and there are a number of calls from Reinholt as well as dozens from the Stryder Clinic."

There was no one in the office at the moment except Paris and she was focused on typing up a report and hadn't so much as looked her way after dropping Tanya's phone records on her desk. Lieutenant Wilson had given her permission to get Tanya's phone records, but she still didn't want him to know that she was working with Brandon to prove Tanya had been murdered and find out who killed her.

"The calls from Reinholt might be something, but it's not unusual for one's employer to call them occasionally."

"How about three dozen times in the last month? And mostly after hours?"

"Okay, that qualifies as unusual. What do you want to do?"

"I need to go speak to Reinholt and then make a stop at the clinic. See if I can't figure out who was making the calls to Tanya and why. Thought you might want to come along."

"I don't have any work that can't wait until later and I can fill you in on my meeting with Morgan Corbett on the way. I'm in."

She smiled into the phone. "Pick you up in ten minutes."

Brandon was waiting when she pulled up in front of his office in a charcoal suit that he looked as if he'd been born to wear.

"How many of those suits do you have?" Yara asked, smoothly pulling the police sedan back onto the street.

Brandon's mouth quirked up into a smile devilish enough to stop traffic. "You're welcome to take a peek in my closet any time."

Heat crawled up her neck. "Just tell me what happened when you talked to Corbett."

He chuckled but began describing his earlier conversation with the assistant district attorney.

"So Zachary Brooks is connected to Tanya. What are the odds?" Yara tapped the brakes, slowing as a teenage male darted across the street against the light.

"Clearly pretty good. Brooks was dating Bailey

Dunlap. Morgan said Zach overheard Tanya and Bailey discussing possible Medicare and prescription fraud. He took the information to the district attorney's office, looking for a deal to get time shaved off his brother's prison sentence."

They stopped at a red light and Yara tapped the steering wheel, thinking. "Brooks is a career criminal. It figures he would have worked out a way to use information like that falling into his lap."

"I suggest we speak to the good doctors," Brandon said.

"Exactly what I was thinking. Right after we talk to Professor Jasper Reinholt."

The parking lot on campus was the size of a soccer field and was nearly full when they parked. The sun was high, but there was still a snap to the air that made it feel colder than the thermometer's report.

"Jasper doesn't have a class listed at this time so we'll have to track him down. His office is in Whitmer Hall to the east of the parking lot."

They set out and found Whitmer Hall easily enough. The building looked like every college brochure, soaring columns and lots of aged stone surrounded by a large, green-grassed quad. Yara knew the campus was not old enough for the building to have actually been built during the century when such architecture would have actually been in vogue. But college students, and more importantly their parents who paid the bills, envisioned a certain university experience and Silver Hill Community College was keen on giving it to them.

They climbed a series of stone stairs and entered the building. There was no directory, but the office doors did have names on them. None of the names on the first several doors were Jasper Reinholt and with four floors in the building, walking the halls to find Reinholt could take some time.

Yara was grateful when the end of the hallway opened up into a small alcove where two women sat behind desks. She supposed they were the professors' assistants and, most likely, the keepers of the most important knowledge on campus.

Neither woman acknowledged their approach.

"Excuse me, could you tell me where I could find Professor Jasper Reinholt's office?" Yara asked.

"Never heard of him," the woman sitting at the desk closest to them said without looking away from her computer. The nameplate on her desk read Rena Smith.

"He's with the anthropology department. This is the sociology floor," the other woman said around the pencil in her mouth. Yara couldn't see if there was a nameplate on her desk.

Yara felt her irritation rising. "Okay, well, what floor are the anthropology professors' offices on?"

Rena sighed, looking away from what she was working on, then gave a little gasp when her eyes fell on Brandon. Her reaction was enough to cause her coworker to stop typing and pay attention as well.

Brandon aimed a dimpled smile at the women. "Ladies, I know how awfully busy you must be taking care of all these insufferable academics. But if you could help my colleague and me out here for just a moment. We're looking for Jasper Reinholt's office. You're correct, he is an anthropology professor."

The woman behind Rena took the pencil out of her mouth as her gaze drank in Brandon. "He'd be on the third floor, then. I'm not sure of his office number," she said with a dazzling smile.

"I can look it up. I've got my building directory right here." Rena reached across her desk, knocking a stack of papers to the floor. She grabbed several sheets of stapled papers that had been stick-pinned to the corkboard on the wall next to her desk. "306B," she said in a tone more appropriate for announcing an Oscar winner than an office number.

"But he's not there." The other woman rose and came to stand next to her colleague's desk, and extended a hand to Brandon, completely ignoring Yara's presence. "I'm Lara."

Brandon took her hand. "It's a pleasure to meet you, Lara."

"Do you know when Professor Reinholt will be back?" Yara asked, fighting to keep the irritation out of her voice.

"No, I mean he's not coming back. Not for a while, at least. The reason I know he's in the anthropology department is that I'm friends with his assistant and she was down here yesterday complaining that Professor Reinholt called the dean yesterday and said he'd be taking a few weeks off for a family emergency effective immediately. As you can imagine, it shook the place up given that the semester had already started and Reinholt gave, like, no notice at all."

"Did he say what the family emergency was?"

"No, at least if he did, he didn't tell Pam. That's his assistant's name. I guess when you have the kind of money he does to fall back on, you don't worry about burning bridges or ticking off your boss."

Yara's ears perked up. "I wasn't aware that Professor Reinholt had any money to speak of."

The two women shot glances at each other.

"Ladies, this is a police investigation. If you know something, now's the time to say it."

The women gave each other another a knowing look and then Lara spoke. "Professor Reinholt doesn't make a big thing about it, but it's not like it is a secret, either. His stepfather is Chauncy St. James, you know, the billionaire tech entrepreneur. He married Professor Reinholt's mother when the professor was a toddler or something so he's basically the man's father. Professor Reinholt makes a big show of living off his salary, driving that hatchback and living in a little house in Kingsborough, but, I mean, it's easy to live like a poor assistant professor when you know you don't really have to."

They thanked the women for their help and then headed to Reinholt's office. As expected, he wasn't in. His assistant was far less forthcoming with information, only sharing that she had no idea when the professor would be back in the office and offering to pass on the message that the police had stopped by to speak with him.

Yara waited until they were back in the car before asking the question that had been on her mind since speaking to the two chatty assistants.

She turned to Brandon without starting the car. "What are the chances that Reinholt just happened to have a family emergency after you asked him questions about his relationship with Tanya?"

"I've never been good at math, but I'd venture to say the odds are low."

She started the car's engine. "Me, too. You have time for a drive by Reinholt's place?"

Brandon graced her with one of his dazzling, dimpled smiles and she felt herself cutting Rena and Lara some slack. It was an ultra sexy smile.

"For you, I have all the time in the world."

Chapter Seventeen

Yara turned on Reinholt's street and searched for his address. The neighborhood seemed familiar and, after a moment, she remembered why. She'd made her first arrest as a cop two streets over years ago. She and her partner had been called to a domestic disturbance where they'd found a man trying to break down the locked bedroom door and get to his wife and child. He'd been hopped up on methamphetamines and it had taken her, her partner and another cop to subdue him. A few weeks after the incident, she'd gotten notice from the district attorney that the charges against the husband were being dropped because his wife was refusing to testify against him.

Despite her initial introduction to it, the neighborhood was a generally safe, run-of-the-mill middle-class enclave. The homes looked well-kept for the most part and there were a fair number of them with signs that young families lived inside, bicycles lying haphazardly on front lawns, swings hanging from the large mature trees in various yards and a virtual bonanza of neutral-colored minivans as far as the eye could see.

She stopped the car in front of a modest Cape Cod with chipping paint and a cracked concrete walkway. "This is Reinholt's place."

"Doesn't look like anyone is home." Brandon peered out of the passenger window. "No car in the driveway."

No car in the driveway and the blinds were pulled on all the windows facing the front of the house.

"Let's go take a closer look." She shut off the engine and met Brandon on the sidewalk.

Brandon glanced up and down the block. "Kind of sad-looking compared to the other houses on the street."

Unlike most of the other homes that virtually burst with signs of the lives being lived inside them, Reinholt's was sterile and bland. Black front door that matched the black shutters and went along with the chipped white siding. Anybody could have lived here. Or nobody, which was what it looked like at the moment.

But she'd been on the job long enough to know that looks could be deceiving and that complacency could get you killed in her line of work. The husband she'd arrested blocks away all those years ago was a mild-mannered accountant when he wasn't hopped up on meth, five foot five and 140 pounds soaking wet, but it had still taken three people to get cuffs on him.

She unsnapped the strap on her holster and shifted

her badge so it could be seen clearly as they approached Reinholt's front door. The sound of drums came from the home to the left while a light from a television screen flashed in the window in the one to the right. Reinholt's place was completely quiet. No sound at all from inside. No interior lights visible through the slats on the blinds.

Yara knocked. "Mr. Reinholt? It's Detective Thomas with the Silver Hill Police Department. Open up, please."

Nothing. She knocked again and peeked through a gap in the blinds on the window closest to the door. Nothing inside the house so much as stirred.

"I don't think he's home," Brandon said, peering through the window on the other side of the door.

"I think you're right. And I get the feeling he hasn't been here for a while."

"He informed the dean about a family emergency yesterday so maybe he's staying with relatives."

"Maybe, if he actually did have a family emergency, and I'm not ready to buy that story."

She rapped on the door again, but without any expectation that the outcome would be any different from the previous two times.

"What now?" Brandon asked.

That was an excellent question.

She turned and looked out over the neighboring houses, thinking. There was something going on with Jasper Reinholt. His lies about the calls and texts to Tanya, holding himself out as an average working Joe when he was really the stepson to one of the richest men in Silver Hill, and now mysteriously disappearing when she wanted to talk to him. He knew more than he was saying. Possibly a lot more. She didn't have nearly enough to officially consider him a suspect in Tanya's death, but she was definitely getting closer to making that leap. And, knowing he was part of one of the most powerful families in town, getting him to talk would likely be all difficult.

She checked her watch, annoyed that Reinholt, at least for now, was a dead end. Lieutenant Wilson wasn't riding her as hard since she'd arrested Brooks for the home invasion robberies, which didn't mean her extended absences would go unnoticed. But she wanted to follow up on the calls that had come from the Stryder Medical Clinic to Tanya after hours enough to risk Lieutenant Wilson's wrath. "Looks like no luck with Reinholt for now."

Brandon strolled beside her. "I can do some digging when I get back to my office. Maybe have Shawn do some as well."

"Your brothers do have a knack for finding out things people want to keep hidden."

Brandon shot her a boyish grin. "It's a living. How about I dig into Reinholt's background, find out everything I can about his family connections and money, and you see if you can't track him down."

"Sounds good." She smiled across the top of the car, reaching for the door handle. "Still have time to take a drive to the clinic and ask the good doctors a few questions?"

Brandon beamed back at her. "I go where you go, Detective."

"Excuse me!"

Brandon turned and Yara shifted to the side so she could see past him to the woman jogging from the house to the right of Reinholt's place.

She was a tall, lanky white woman in black leggings, an oversize sweatshirt and running shoes. Her hair was up in a sweaty knot at the top of her head.

"I don't mean to pry, but I saw you coming from Jasper's house and, well, I watch enough *Law & Order* to recognize an unmarked police sedan when I see one." The woman chuckled. "I'm Marion Knight, Jasper's neighbor. I just wanted to make sure everything is okay." Her brow creased with worry. "I saw Jasper take off out of here yesterday like a bat out of you know where. He didn't even stop when I called out to him."

Yara circled the car and came to stand in front of the woman on the sidewalk in front of her house. "You saw Jasper leave his house last night? Around what time?"

"Oh, seven, maybe a little after. *Wheel of Fortune* had just come on so it couldn't have been too much later than that."

Yara's eyes flicked to the woman's house, where the television could still be seen through the window. She didn't know one game show from the other, but it appeared that a contestant was spinning a large stand-up wheel on whichever one was on at the moment.

"Did Jasper have anything with him when he left?"

"Anything? Oh, like a suitcase. I think so. He threw something across the car into the passenger seat after he opened the door, like he had a duffel bag or something. He was moving pretty quickly so I didn't get a good look."

"Does he often take off like that, unexpectedly?" Brandon asked.

Marion shook her head. "I can't say that he does. At least not that I've ever noticed before."

And since Yara got the sense that Marion noticed just about everything that happened on the block, it was safe to say that Reinholt didn't take off often.

Which meant nothing. He could have still gotten a call about a family emergency. In fact, everything Marion was telling them was consistent with that.

"Have you noticed Mr. Reinholt acting differently lately? Has he been angry or upset?"

Marion looked taken aback by the question. She actually physically took a step away from them. "No, I mean, not that I've noticed. Jasper is a good neighbor, but we aren't close. We speak, just to say 'hello,' you know, if we both happen to be outside at the same time."

Yara pulled her phone out of her pocket and flipped until she found a photograph of Tanya. "Have you seen this woman at Mr. Reinholt's home in the last month?"

Marion studied the phone screen for several seconds before shaking her head. "I can't say that I have. Sorry. What is all this about? Is Jasper in some trouble?"

Yara smiled tightly. "Thank you, Ms. Knight. You've been very helpful."

Marion frowned, likely not missing the fact that Yara hadn't answered her question. "If you really want to find Jasper, you should try his job. He is dedicated to educating the next generation."

"Thanks, we'll do that." Yara pulled a business card from her pocket. "If you do see Mr. Reinholt, could you let him know Detective Thomas is looking for him? And if you remember anything else that you think could be helpful, please give me a call."

Marion took the card, then turned and went back inside her house.

Yara turned to Brandon. "What do you think? Is Reinholt our guy?"

Brandon's shoulders went up, then back down. "He's certainly acting suspicious, but it could be just what it looks like. A family emergency called him away."

Yara started around the car again. "Yeah, or he could be a murderer on the run."

YARA HAD TO circle the clinic's parking lot twice before she spotted a car backing out of a space. They parked in it, then climbed from the car and headed for the clinic.

"Dr. Manning is not going to be happy to see us," Brandon said.

"Good. I'm not happy to be here. I'm sick of people lying and keeping things from me. I'm trying to find a killer and all anyone is concerned with is keeping their silly secrets."

She pulled open the door to the clinic and a blast of warm air hit them as they approached the reception area. A young man wearing a headset complete with microphone sat behind the desk.

"I'm Detective Thomas. I'm here to see Dr. Manning."

"Do you have an appointment?"

Yara's smile was almost feral. "No, but we would appreciate the doctor making the time."

The receptionist gave them a pitying look. "I'm sure you understand Dr. Manning is very busy. Maybe you'd like to make an appointment."

"If I make an appointment it will be with a judge. For a warrant to turn this place inside out."

The receptionist's eyes widened with fear. "One moment, please." He tapped four numbers on the phone's keyboard and swiveled his chair away from them. The space was small so they could hear his conversation. Dr. Manning wasn't happy, but the receptionist's repetition of Yara's threat to get a warrant seemed to do the trick.

The receptionist swung back to them with a faux smile on his face. "The doctor will see you now. Down the hall and to the left."

The door to Dr. Manning's office was cracked open. Brandon knocked, then pushed the door open wider. He was on the phone, his already gloomy expression darkening when Yara and Brandon entered.

"I've got to call you back," Manning said to the person on the other end of the line.

He put the phone down and straightened in his high-backed chair. "Detective Thomas." He nodded at Yara. "And I don't believe we've met as yet," he said, his gaze raking over Brandon.

"This is my associate, Brandon West. Thank you for seeing us without an appointment."

"I didn't see that I had much choice. Not with the threats you were making."

"Not threats, Doctor. Just making it clear what steps I'd be forced to take if you weren't able to speak with me."

"Call it what you want, but I don't appreciate you barging in here like this. I'm only indulging you because I want, as much as anyone, to know the truth about what happened to poor Tanya. Her family deserves that."

"I'm glad you feel that way, Doctor. Then you won't have any problem explaining why you didn't tell me and Detective Rachlin about the federal government's ongoing investigation into the clinic."

Dr. Manning darted a nervous look around the office. "That's not relevant to what happened to Tanya."

"And how do you know that?" Yara pressed.

"Because the whole investigation is nonsense," Manning said with false bluster.

"The feds got a tip that doctors working at this clinic have been selling prescription drugs to patients and nonpatients. That doesn't sound like nonsense to me."

"Well, it is. None of the doctors I work with would ever violate their oaths like that. It's outrageous that anyone would take the word of an anonymous tipster over the words of two well-respected doctors in the community."

"It's funny that you mention an anonymous tip. I didn't think much information about the investigation had been released. How did you know the investigation was opened based on an anonymous tip?"

"Well, I..." The doctor shifted in his chair uncomfortably. "As I said, the whole investigation is nonsense, and I have many friends who understand that and don't want to see this clinic or my reputation tarnished."

"So you have someone feeding you information on the investigation?"

Manning huffed out a breath. "Is this really what you came here to talk to me about?"

"Did you suspect Tanya of being the anonymous source?"

Manning clenched his teeth, his gaze skittering away. "No."

"Very convincing," Brandon deadpanned. "So did you ask Tanya if she'd contacted the authorities, Tanya's bosses or the medical board?"

"I told you—"

"You lied," Yara interrupted. "And I'm getting pretty sick of being lied to. Maybe it makes more sense to get that warrant. Search this place for the answers I'm looking for myself." She stood and Brandon followed suit.

It actually wasn't easy to get a warrant to search a doctor's office and Yara doubted she had enough to get a judge to grant one, but the threat seemed to have the desired effect on Manning.

Manning popped up out of his chair. "Wait. Wait."

"Doctor, I'm at the end of my patience. Cooperation or a search warrant. What is it going to be?"

Manning looked beaten. "Okay, look, I suspected Tanya was the person who went to the authorities. She came to me with concerns about Dr. Gristedes. She thought he was prescribing medication to patients who didn't really need it and miscoding some procedures."

"And what did you do about her assertion?" Brandon asked.

"I told her that the doctors prescribed medication, not the nurses. I have the utmost confidence in Dr. Gristedes's diagnostic skills. I don't think it is appropriate for the support staff to second-guess a doctor."

"So your theory is that Tanya contacted the authorities after you blew off her suspicions?" Yara pushed back.

"Who else could it have been? This clinic has been serving the community for nearly twenty years and suddenly, after Tanya Rutger begins working here, these scurrilous charges are hurled at us. I'd actually hoped that after Tanya's death this baseless investigation might be dropped."

Yara's lips curled with disgust at the man in front of her. "Is there anything else you haven't told us?"

Manning glared. "I've told you everything I know."

She and Brandon headed for Gristedes's office, but it was dark and empty.

Yara tried the doctor's cell but got no answer.

They had better luck when it came to finding Bailey. She was in the staff lounge having a cup of coffee with another nurse. At the sight of Yara's badge, the second nurse excused herself, shooting an ominous look over her shoulder at Bailey before she left the room.

Yara settled in the chair Bailey's coworker had just vacated while Brandon took the other empty chair at the table. Bailey chewed her bottom lip, her gaze trained on the mug between her hands.

"Bailey, you lied to me."

Bailey lifted her head. "No, I didn't lie."

"You didn't tell me that Tanya thought your bosses were engaged in fraud and illegal prescription sales."

Bailey's face reddened. "I…I didn't think it had anything to do with Tanya's suicide."

"You also didn't tell me you were dating Zachary Brooks."

Her face scrunched in confusion. "Zach? I'm not dating him."

"But you were. And while you were dating him, Tanya told you about the doctors at the Stryder Medical Clinic engaging in Medicare fraud and selling illegal prescriptions."

Bailey's eyes darted to the door, fear swimming in

them. She leaned forward and dropped her voice to a whisper. "Do we have to discuss this here? Now?"

"Yes." But in deference to the sensitive situation that Bailey was in and in the hope of getting her to talk, Yara dropped her voice to a whisper as well. "This is a murder investigation. The murder of your friend."

"Murder?" Bailey pressed her hand against her chest. "I thought Tanya killed herself."

"We no longer think that's the case." At least she no longer thought it. And when Lieutenant Wilson found out she was pursuing the case as a homicide, there would be hell to pay, which was why she needed to have a suspect by the time he realized what she'd been doing. "That's why it's even more important now that you tell me the whole truth."

Bailey swallowed hard. "I…I can't believe this."

"Were you and Zachary Brooks dating?" Yara pressed.

Bailey hesitated for a moment before nodding. "*Dating* is probably too strong a word for it. We hooked up for a few weeks before I realized what a loser he was."

At least she'd realized it, Yara thought. "During the period you were hooking up, did Tanya come to you with her suspicion that your employer was committing Medicare fraud and the illegal prescriptions?"

Bailey shrugged and looked down at the table again. "Yeah, but I thought she was way off base and I told her so. I mean, maybe the doctors prescribed medications to some patients who didn't really need it, but all doctors do it, right? It's like the dirty little secret of the profession and it doesn't really hurt anyone. The patients are asking for the medication."

"You have an obligation to report them to the bosses and board," Brandon said, disdain lacing his words.

Yara shot him a sharp look. She didn't want Bailey to stop talking to them.

Bailey glared. "I also have an obligation to pay the rent every month. I need my job. Best-case scenario, the medical board pulls the doctor's license, the practice shuts down and no other practice will hire the nurse who ratted on her prior employers. Worst-case scenario, no one believes me, I get fired and no other practice will hire the nurse who ratted on her prior employers. Either way, I get screwed."

She wasn't off base. That was pretty close to what had happened when Tanya took her suspicions to Dr. Manning. She'd been slapped down without so much as a cursory investigation into her suspicions.

"Anyway, we thought Tanya had let it go," Bailey said.

"We?" Yara pressed.

"Zach and I."

"So Zach knew about Tanya's suspicions?" Brandon questioned.

"Yeah, he overheard us arguing about what she should do and wanted to know what we were talking about."

Yara had her notebook out and was taking notes. "Think back. When was this?"

Bailey cocked her head, her expression thoughtful. "I don't know exactly. We weren't together long, but we were pretty hot and heavy while we were together. He was around all the time for about a month. Maybe a little more."

"Okay," Yara said, frustrated. "Did Zach seem overly interested in Tanya's accusations?"

"I think he might have asked her some questions, like she was really worked up about it. She wanted to go to the medical board."

"And what did Zach think about that?"

"He was on the same page with me. The world doesn't treat men like Doc Manning and Doc Gristedes like it does the rest of us. We told Tanya she should just mind her own business. She never brought it up again so I thought she decided we were right."

But Tanya hadn't let it go. She knew what the doctors were doing was wrong and exploitative, and she wanted to put a stop to it. And it looked like it might have cost her life.

"You know, one thing was weird, now that I think about it," Bailey said suddenly.

"What?" Yara asked. "One time when Zach came to pick me up from work, I did see him talking to Dr. Gristedes in the parking lot when I came out."

Yara shared a glance with Brandon. "Was this after Zach knew about Tanya's accusations?"

Bailey's nose crinkled in thought. "I think so. Yeah, it was. I remember. I got worried and I asked what they'd been talking about and Zach said he'd just asked if the guy had a cigarette and that Dr.

Gristedes had given him a whole speech about how bad smoking was for his health."

"So it's possible Zach didn't know he was talking to your boss?"

Bailey shrugged again. "It's possible. The doctors didn't usually wear their lab coats out of the office."

"But you don't believe that?" Brandon pressed her.

"All I know is that Zach turned out to be not at all the nice guy he seemed to be at first. I wouldn't put anything past him."

Zachary Brooks was definitely not a nice guy. And Yara was willing to bet that his chat with Dr. Gristedes was about more than the perils of smoking.

Zach had traded the information he'd learned about the doctor's possible crimes to the district attorney. Who's to say he hadn't also tried playing both sides against each other. Maybe earn a few bucks from the doctor in exchange for warning him about Tanya's suspicions. Maybe he'd even offered to take care of the doctor's problem for him. He'd already gotten away with attempted murder. Maybe he figured he could beat the rap again. The problem was she didn't have anything that directly implicated Zach or Dr. Manning and Dr. Gristedes in Tanya's murder.

She and Brandon headed back to the parking lot.

Brandon stopped in front of the car. "You look frustrated."

"I am. I know in my gut that Tanya didn't kill herself, but this case is nothing but a web of lies and razor-thin connections leading to nowhere."

He put a hand on each of her shoulders and turned her to face him. "Then we'll just have to cut through that web and build out those connections. I trust your gut, Yara. I trust you."

Desire crackled between them.

She stepped back before she did something truly foolish like kiss Brandon West in a public parking lot for the world to see.

Brandon frowned, but turned and walked around the car to the passenger side and got in. "May I suggest we stop by the West Investigations offices and update my brothers on what we've discovered today?"

"I don't like the idea of reading your brothers in on this."

"They are a resource, Yara. One we need. This off-the-books investigation has gotten more complicated, as you noted, web of lies and all," he reminded her pointedly. "We need all the help we can get."

He wasn't wrong. She could feel time running out. Eventually, Lieutenant Wilson would figure out what she'd been up to. She had to have something by then or her career would go up in flames.

"Okay. Maybe West Investigations will have better luck tracking down Jasper Reinholt." She put the car in gear and pulled out of the parking spot.

Brandon removed his phone from his suit jacket pocket. "I'll call and let them know we're on our way. And I'm sure they have their own contacts in the attorney general's office. Maybe they'll be able to get us more details about the investigation into the doctors at Stryder Medical and Zach's role as a material witness."

She hoped so because right now they needed to catch a break.

Chapter Eighteen

The headquarters for West Security and Investigations was located in Harlem, not far from where Brandon and his brothers had grown up. Yara parked in the garage two blocks from the offices where West rented several parking spaces and had a validated parking arrangement for its VIP clients. As they walked to the building, Brandon couldn't help but reflect on how familiar the neighborhood was and how many memories just the short walk between the garage and West's offices brought back. As much as he loved his town house in the suburbs, there would always be a part of him that called Harlem home.

His call had paved the way and the receptionist wasted no time upon their arrival leading them to a conference room where Ryan and Shawn waited. He made the introductions, then pulled out a chair for Yara at the conference table, waiting until she'd settled before he took the seat next to her.

Ryan and Shawn West sat on the other side of the long glass-top conference room table. Brandon looked across the table at his brothers, the family resemblance among the three of them stark in such close quarters.

He shot a look at Yara out of the corner of his eye, wondering whether she'd vote him the handsomest West brother out of the three she'd met, or had one of his younger brothers captured that honor?

He pushed the prick of jealousy away. Now wasn't the time.

"Brandon's told us a little about the investigation you two are working on but it seems like you've run into some trouble," Ryan said.

Yara shot him a look that seemed to say this was his show, so he took the lead. "We've learned a lot of new information in the last twenty-four hours but we've also hit a bit of a dead end."

Shawn leaned forward. "Tell us about it."

He caught his brothers up on Zachary Brooks's arrest and the subsequent discovery of his role in the investigation into Medicare fraud and illegal prescription sales by the doctors at the Stryder Medical Clinic and Tanya's ex, Jasper Reinholt, and his sudden disappearance.

"Looks like you two have covered a lot of ground," Ryan said, looking impressed. "How can we help?"

"The medical examiner came back with a preliminary finding of suicide, so my boss has written this case off," Yara answered.

Shawn cocked his head. "Clearly you don't agree with your boss."

"I do not, but I do want to keep my job."

"We need you to look into Jasper Reinholt. Find out where he's gone," Brandon said.

Ryan wrote the name on the legal pad on the table in front of him. "That shouldn't be too hard. What do you know about him?"

Yara laid out everything they had on Jasper—his address, employer and everything they knew about his relationship with Tanya.

"It would also be great if you could take a deeper dive into the Stryder Medical Clinic and the lives of Dr. Manning and Dr. Gristedes. Tanya thought Gristedes was involved in the fraud and illegal prescriptions and I definitely don't trust Dr. Manning. And see if there's any connection between the doctors that run the clinic, Manning and Gristedes, and the career criminal, Zachary Brooks."

Ryan's right hand moved quickly over the paper, jotting notes.

Yara's cell phone rang. She pulled it from her purse and frowned. "Excuse me. I need to take this."

She stepped into the hallway before connecting the call. Through the glass wall, he could see that the frown remained on her face.

"Anything else we can do for you?" Shawn said drolly, pulling Brandon's attention back to his brothers.

"Actually, there is. Someone, a man, prepaid a year of Tanya's rent on a one-bedroom luxury apartment in the Financial District."

Brandon gave Shawn the description of the man who had been with Tanya when she rented the apartment.

Ryan looked up from his notes, frowning. "That is not a lot to go on."

"I know, but it's all we have," Brandon said.

"We'll do what we can, but no promises."

"That's all I can ask." He left his brothers still sitting at the table.

Yara punched off her call as he exited the conference room. "Everything is okay."

"Yeah, just my brother's babysitter had a family emergency. My brother is a single dad and is an independent electrician and he's about an hour away on a house call. I need to head over to his house to watch my niece, Sasha, until he gets home."

"Okay, well, I'm sure someone here can give me a ride back to my office."

"Or you can come with me."

He was equal parts surprised and ecstatic at the offer.

"Unless you have to get back to work, which I totally understand," Yara added quickly.

There was no way he was letting her back out of the offer now. He grinned. "I'd love to."

YARA SPENT THE short drive to her brother's Cape Cod home in the neighborhood where they'd grown up waffling over whether bringing Brandon with her was a good idea. On the one hand, he'd seemed more than willing to jump into babysitting duty with her, which was endearing. She wasn't sure she'd ever have children. She didn't think it was fair when she had such a dangerous job. But she loved Sasha as if she were her own. On the other hand, she was giving him a glimpse into her life that she'd never given any other man. She'd never even brought a boyfriend home. Not that she'd kept any around long enough to make it a holiday.

Yet, she'd invited Brandon to meet Sasha and it felt…right.

She couldn't deny it any longer. Not to herself at least. She was falling for Brandon West.

Her six-year-old niece, Sasha, was waiting for her on the porch with Mrs. Hannigan, Eddie's regular after-school babysitter. Sasha stood next to the older woman in sparkly tennis shoes, jean skirt, blue tights, a pink shirt and her hair in a poof-ponytail at the top of her head.

Sasha jumped off the porch and raced toward Yara as she rounded the front of the car. "Hey, kid. How's it going?" She scooped her niece into her arms and planted a kiss on her chubby cheek.

Sasha placed a sticky hand on either side of her face and smacked an equally sticky kiss on Yara's lips. "It's going good, Auntie Yara. Miss Hanny is making cookies with me."

"I'm so sorry." Jessica Hannigan met them beside the car. "My mother's taken a fall. Her neighbor found her in the kitchen and called an ambulance. She's on her way to the hospital now. I wouldn't abandon Sasha for anything, but…"

Yara reached out and squeezed the woman's shoulder. "Jess, don't worry about Sasha. I've got her. You just go be with your mother."

Jessica swiped a tear from her face. "Thank you." She hurried toward the red van parked in the driveway.

"Let us know if we can do anything. Eddie and I are here for you," Yara called out to the woman's retreating back.

"Auntie Yara?"

"Yes, sweetie?"

"Who is he?" Sasha pointed at Brandon.

"My name is Brandon." He extended a hand to her niece. "What's your name?"

Never a shy child, Sasha grabbed Brandon's hand and shook it up and down like a noodle. "Sasha. What are you doing with my aunt Yara?"

Brandon shot her a glee-filled look.

"Brandon is a friend. Let's get back inside." She lowered Sasha to the ground.

"We have more cookies to bake." Sasha ran for the house.

"Do you know how to bake cookies?" Brandon asked as they followed Sasha.

"How hard can it be?"

Yara's brother, Eddie, had purchased the three-bedroom bungalow, a fixer-upper, four years ago after his wife decided she wasn't cut out to be a full-time mother and wife. An electrician who often worked unpredictable hours, Eddie became a single father overnight. Yara did as much as she could to help her brother and be a strong female figure in her niece's life. And, although their parents had passed away years ago, they were lucky enough to live in a community that was eager to step up and help. Case in point: Jessica Hannigan had been Yara and Eddie's babysitter while they were growing up. Now she did the daily pickup for Sasha and pinch-hit on nights when Eddie got emergency late-night callouts.

The kitchen looked like a tornado had blown through. Sugar, eggs, vanilla, butter, salt, baking soda, brown sugar, flour and chocolate chips were strewn across the small island countertop.

Sasha pulled on her hand. "Auntie Yara, I need four dozen for the bake fair tomorrow."

Yara scanned the mess for a recipe. "Sasha, where's the recipe?"

Sasha's narrow shoulders went up, then down. "I dunno. Miss Hanny just told me what to do, but I can't use the mixer by myself."

Panic fluttered in her stomach. Point her in the direction of a fleeing suspect and she'd run him to ground, but baking? The kitchen really was not her domain. She looked at Brandon.

He was holding back a laugh. "Don't worry. I got this." He clapped his hands together and went down on his haunches so he'd be eye to eye with Sasha. "Chocolate chip cookies are my favorite."

"No eating!" Sasha admonished.

"Not even a tiny, tiny little cookie?" Brandon held his index finger and thumb a half an inch apart.

"No."

"What if we make extra and eat those?"

Sash cocked her head to the side in thought. "I guess that would be okay."

"Let's get to it, then." Brandon extended his hand. Sasha took it and he helped her onto the step stool already placed in front of the island.

"What did Jess plan for dinner?" Given her brother's schedule and the early dinner time of a six-year-old, Jess usually made sure Sasha ate.

"Spaghetti." Sasha pointed to the box of angel-hair pasta and jar of tomato sauce next to the sink.

"Okay, I'll get that started while you two make the cookies."

Brandon and Sasha got to work, her niece enthusiastically walking Brandon through a minute-by-minute replay of a day in the life of a kindergartner. To his credit, Brandon patiently directed Sasha in combining and mixing the cookie ingredients and listened with rapt attention as she talked.

She wasn't a woman who pined for children. She loved being an auntie to Sasha and if she never had children of her own that would be enough. But watching Brandon interact with her niece, how good he was with her, Yara couldn't help but wonder what he'd be like with his own kids. Kids who were his... and hers.

Annnnnd she was letting her imagination run wild. She blamed it on the scene of perfect domesticity that she appeared to be caught up in at the moment. In reality, she was a cop. And cops and marriage and families did not mix well.

She prepared the spaghetti, one of the few meals

she actually knew how to make. By the time Eddie walked through the front door a little more than an hour after she and Brandon arrived, dinner was ready and the last batch of cookies was in the oven.

Yara introduced the two men, ignoring the smug grin that spread across her brother's face as she did. She was in for some teasing from her little brother.

"Thanks for taking care of the cookies. I totally forgot," Eddie said, gently loosening Sasha's grip on his neck. Sasha had jumped on her daddy the moment he'd walked through the door, wrapping herself around him.

"Brandon helped me because Auntie Yara didn't know how."

"Way to support the sisterhood, kid." Yara tweaked her niece's thigh. "Okay, you guys' dinner is ready for you on the stove. Brandon and I are going to head out."

"Why don't you stay for dinner." Eddie looked from her to Brandon and back. If she didn't know better, she'd think it was nothing more than a polite offer, but she knew her brother. She could see the curiosity burning behind his eyes.

"I don't think—"

"We'd love to," Brandon interrupted. He gave her a shrug. "I didn't have lunch and we're here."

Her stomach rumbled loudly at that moment, reminding her that Brandon wasn't the only one who hadn't found time to eat lunch that day.

Eddie lifted the top on the pot with the pasta. "Yeah, sis, stay. You made far too much pasta for two people anyway. Sasha and I will need help eating all this."

"Please, Auntie Yara?" Sasha whined.

Yara knew when she was beat. "Okay. Spaghetti for four coming up."

Brandon and Sasha took the last batch of cookies from the oven while she and Eddie grabbed plates and silverware.

"New boyfriend? Is it serious?" her brother whispered as he helped her set the table.

"Shh." She glanced through the opening separating the kitchen from the small formal dining area. "He's not a boyfriend. We're barely friends."

Eddie smiled teasingly. "You two looked very domestic when I walked in. Are you sure you don't want to give up chasing the bad guys, settle down and pop out a few ornery mini-Yaras?"

Sasha skipped into the room.

"Can we not discuss this right now?" Yara hissed.

Sasha tipped her head, eyeing them solemnly. "It's not nice to whisper when other people are in the room."

"You are quite right, Sasha. So what are you two talking about?" Brandon said entering the dining room with the bowl of angel-hair pasta in one hand and the tomato sauce in the other.

Yara pulled out the nearest chair and sat. "I was just saying how famished I am. Let's eat."

Brandon fit right in with her family, keeping up the dinner conversation with both Eddie and Sasha. She hadn't expected the tornado of feelings that hit her as she'd watched Brandon and Sasha baking cookies.

Because she'd determined it would be selfish to bring another person into her life when her job meant she might not come home one day, much less bring children into such a situation, she'd never given much thought to what having a family of her own would actually look like. But when she was bustling around Eddie's kitchen fixing dinner, listening to the banter between Brandon and Sasha, she'd let herself envision, for the briefest of moments, what it might feel like if Brandon was her husband and the child he was baking with was theirs. And it felt…right.

A mixture of fear and exhilaration churned in her stomach. She glanced across the table, her gaze meeting Brandon's, which was already fixed on her. A buzz of sexual awareness sparked through her.

You okay? he mouthed silently.

She realized she'd been holding her fork inches from her mouth for who knows how long.

Okay was relative. At the moment, her head was filled with visions of babies with the same piercing brown eyes that stared at her from across the table. And, more specifically, the process of making those babies.

But she just nodded and focused on her spaghetti.

Over the course of working with Brandon, something had changed. Somehow, while she wasn't paying attention, he'd burrowed his way into her life and now she was having a hard time imagining a future without him in it. And she was pretty sure she didn't want to.

The revelation rocked her to her core.

Brandon was unlike any man she'd ever known. A lawyer, yes. She still didn't love the profession, but he cared about justice and doing what was right. He was a man who cared about other people—his family, his community, her.

And as hard as she'd tried not to, she cared about him. Deeply.

Enough to consider bending her rules about getting into a serious relationship. Heck, whom was she kidding? She was thinking about throwing that rule into the dumpster and setting it aflame.

As if he knew what she was thinking, Brandon's lips turned up into a sexy grin that set *her* aflame.

She avoided making eye contact with him for the rest of dinner and the twin smirks on her brother's and Brandon's faces let her know that it hadn't gone unnoticed.

Eddie refused to let her and Brandon help with the cleanup when they were finished, shooing them out of the house.

They walked side by side down the driveway to her car, the tension between them somehow growing thicker in the night air than it was inside the house. A half-moon shone in the sky and crickets chirped a discordant tune.

She moved to walk around the front of the car to the driver's side.

Brandon's hand shot out, stopping her, drawing

her close. The hand around her wrist moved to her waist while he cupped her cheek with his other hand. He lowered his mouth to hers and she stepped in closer, immediately deepening the kiss.

She wanted him with every cell in her body. Tasting him, feeling the pressure of his body against hers, it awakened a need she'd been denying for too long. A need that only Brandon could fulfill. And if the hunger she felt in his kisses was any indication, he was feeling the same as she was. He was driving her wild and they were only kissing. She might not make it to morning if she listened to her body and spent the night with him.

But what a way to go.

Brandon broke off the kiss. "We might want to take this somewhere more private before one of your brother's neighbors calls your coworkers on us."

"Your place?"

His lips turned up into a wolfish grin and desire flashed in his eyes. "You drive."

Chapter Nineteen

She didn't let herself think about anything other than the pleasure she was in for on the short drive to Brandon's house. From the tightness of his pants, he was thinking about the same thing. Good. She wasn't going to overthink or analyze this. They wanted each other and, for tonight at least, that was enough.

Five more minutes and then they'd be at his place. She pressed down on the accelerator, thinking that was five minutes too long.

She parked the car behind his BMW in his short driveway three and a half minutes later and shut off the engine. Hand in hand, they walked to the door and he let her enter first.

She entered without hesitation and when he shut the door, flicking the lock while backing her against the door, she didn't resist. She smiled.

His kiss was firm. His spicy male scent caused desire to flare within her. She parted her lips and he deepened the kiss, exploring her mouth. He pulled her closer and she slid her arms around his neck. She wanted him. Right here and now. She glided her hands over the front of his shirt and around his shoulders, loving the feel of his hard muscles.

He pulled his mouth from hers and she felt the absence so acutely she moaned.

The desire she felt was reflected in his eyes. "Are you sure?"

She didn't hesitate. "Yes. Absolutely. I want you."

This time the sound came from deep in his chest. He took her mouth again and she sank into him.

His hands moved down her sides and he gripped her hips, molding their bodies together.

Every cell in her body shivered with anticipation. Their kisses alternated between soft and searching and deep and needy. And she couldn't get enough.

"Hold on." His arms tightened again and he lifted her off her feet and turned toward the stairs. She wrapped her legs around his waist, grinding her pelvis against his.

He groaned. "We're not going to make it to the bedroom if you keep doing that."

She laughed and did it again. "It's a risk I'm willing to take."

Brandon slapped her gently on the bottom and kept moving. They kissed their way up the staircase and made it into his bedroom.

He set her feet on the floor and snaked his hand up under her shirt while leaving a trail of hot kisses along her neck. She gave a low hum in response.

He explored every inch of her, his hands roaming over her breasts, her hips, down the side of her thigh and then up again toward her core. He pushed her bra to the side and brought his lips back to her body.

"I've wanted to do this since the moment I saw you."

"It took me a little longer to get here, to be honest with you," she said breathlessly.

"Oh, it did, did it? I think I'll have to make you pay for that little jab." She pulled her shirt over her head and unfastened her bra, tossing both onto a chair in the corner of the room.

His mouth went right to her breast, sending shivers rippling through her body.

"I think I'm going to like my punishment," she said, nearly breathless.

"I think you will, too." He walked her backward until the back of her legs hit the bed. "Lie back."

She followed his instructions.

He pulled his own shirt over his head, then slid his hands over her waistband and undid the button, slowly easing down the zipper while he watched her with a look so intent it made her body flush.

Her heart thundered with anticipation. She raised her hips and he slid the pants free of her legs.

He eased down onto the bed next to her, kissing her deeply. She ran her hands over his chest and pulled him close.

He traced a finger from her breast to her navel and lower, making her insides tighten. He eased her panties from her hips and then chucked the rest of his clothes while she watched.

Gently, he eased on top of her, settling between her thighs.

He kissed her again deeply, pressing her into the bed. Her body throbbed with want.

His body felt like heaven on top of hers. He kissed down her neck to her shoulders before lavishing attention on each of her breasts in turn. He lingered there until she was in danger of losing her mind.

She arched against him. "Brandon, please. I need you."

Then he moved lower, driving her over the edge.

He leaned across her and opened a drawer in the nightstand while she came down. He sheathed himself, then pushed into her.

She moaned with the pleasure of it. Feeling him sit himself deep inside her, she wrapped her legs around him and pulled him deeper.

They found a rhythm quickly, the tension building inside her for a second time. "Brandon. Brandon, you feel so good."

"So do you, baby. I don't know how much longer I can hang on."

But it didn't matter because a moment later she crested again and he followed right behind her.

He rolled onto his back and pulled her in close to his side.

She turned onto her side, fighting to catch her breath. She ran her hand lightly over his chest, kissed his shoulder.

"That was spectacular," he said.

"Amazing."

He dropped a kiss on her head, then pushed up from the bed and went into the adjoining bathroom. He was back moments later, drawing her back into his arms.

"Stay the night. Don't think. Just say yes."

She laughed, relaxed to the point of giddy from what he'd just done to her body. "Is this how you sweet-talk all your conquests?"

He shifted, looking into her eyes. "You aren't a conquest. I want to wake up with you in my arms. Say yes."

Her chest tightened with an emotion she couldn't name. She wasn't sure she wanted to try to name it at the moment. She just wanted to enjoy the feeling of being in his arms.

"Yes." She closed her eyes and tucked her head against his chest.

They fell asleep in each other's arms.

BRANDON AWOKE TO Yara's arm draped over his torso, her warm body pressed into his side. Her head rested against his shoulder and her chest rose and fell rhythmically. This was the most relaxed he'd seen her since, well, a few hours earlier when she'd been coming down from their second, or maybe their third, round of lovemaking.

Love.

Damn. He'd be the first to admit he'd wanted to take her to bed since she strode into the courthouse and demanded he tell her everything he knew about Tanya Rutger. Hell, he'd wanted her in his bed since last year. But he'd had every intention of keeping emotions out of the equation. And at that he'd failed miserably because he could no longer deny it, not to himself anyway.

He was in love with Yara Thomas.

The thought made his heart thump uncontrollably in his chest.

Yara opened her eyes and a slow, sensual smile spread across her luscious mouth. "Hi."

"Good morning." He pressed a kiss to her lips but she drew back quickly.

"Uh, I haven't brushed."

"I don't care," he said, going for another kiss.

After a long moment, Yara broke away again. She ran a finger along his stubbled jaw, sending electric currents to his groin. This woman was going to kill him, but what a way to go.

He shifted, pressing her back to the mattress with every intention of going for round four.

Yara wiggled away with a giggle, a sound he never would have expected to hear from her before last night. Now it was a sound he was determined to draw from her as often as possible.

"I have to go home and get ready for work." She pressed a hand to his chest to stop him from pressing his body to hers in the way that every cell of his being cried out for.

"What I have in mind is a lot more fun than work." He rained kisses down her neck while his hand traveled low, grazing along her hip.

His touch elicited a moan from her that set his libido aflame.

A crash and the sound of glass shattering had them both stilling for a split second before Brandon jumped from the bed. He had an advantage over Yara, having pulled on a pair of pajama bottoms prior to their falling into a satiated slumber hours earlier.

It only took a second to grab the gun he kept for protection from the safe hidden away in the nightstand next to his bed, then he bounded down the stairs.

Glass littered the rug in the rarely used formal living room at the front of the house. A red brick lay next to a cylindrical tube in the middle of the shattered glass. It looked like someone had thrown a brick through the window, then followed it up with a smoke bomb. The vapor was filling the small room quickly and would move to the rest of the house if he didn't do something.

He waded forward, grabbed the tube and tossed it through the broken window out onto the porch. Not ideal, but a smoke bomb was more nuisance than harmful.

He could hear Yara's footsteps beating the stair treads. "Be careful. There's glass everywhere."

She joined him in the living room. She'd pulled on the clothes she'd worn to his house, her yellow dress shirt buttoned haphazardly and untucked. Her service weapon was in her hand. "I can see that and it looks like you cut yourself." She pointed to his foot.

Drops of blood joined the glass on the light-colored

rug, likely ruining it. He hadn't felt the tiny sliver that protruded from the side of his foot until she'd pointed it out, but now the sting radiated through his foot.

He swore and hobbled to the kitchen. He set his gun on the counter, then fell onto one of the bar stools and pressed a napkin against the gash. "It's not bad. Nothing some antiseptic and a bandage won't take care of."

"Whoever did this will need more than a bandage when I get through with them."

"One of the Stryder doctors?" he asked.

"Or Reinholt. I have no doubt this has everything to do with the investigation into Tanya's murder."

"I'd say so. I've lived here for nearly two years and I haven't had any trouble until now. Someone is scared," he said.

"Or desperate. Either way, this is a major escalation. They've attacked your home. It could be dangerous for you."

He shot her a pointed look. "This might not have been about me, or at least not all about me. Your car is in the driveway. Whoever did this could have known that you were here. They may have followed us."

Yara shook her head. "From my brother's house? Doubtful."

But he could see the fear in her eyes. He took great pains to keep his home address under wraps. Technically, the town house was owned by an LLC. It wasn't impossible to discover he was the sole member of that LLC, but it was far more likely that whoever was behind this had followed him or Yara at some point and found out where he lived.

"You're probably right," he said, more in hopes of dimming the fear he saw in her eyes than because he actually believed what he was saying.

"This was a bad idea. Letting you get involved in this. I don't know what I was thinking." She paced in front of him.

He stood and took her by the shoulders. "You didn't let me get involved. I would have gotten involved with or without you." He crouched a bit so he could look directly into her eyes. "Don't bail on me now. We're getting close to answers. I know it."

"You could have been hurt." Emotion swam in her eyes.

For a moment, he dared to dream it might be... No, he knew how he felt about Yara, but he wouldn't rush her. He'd give her however much time she needed to realize they were meant to be together. Just as long as they could be in each other's lives while she figured it out.

"You could have been hurt, too, but neither of us were. Let's just be thankful for that."

"I'm not going to let you get hurt," she replied, pulling him closer and resting her head against his chest.

The sound of sirens cut through the night.

Yara disappeared into the living room and returned seconds later. "Looks like one of your neighbors called 911."

Brandon swept his eyes over her. "Since your colleagues appear to be on their way, you might want to make yourself look a little less comfortable."

Yara swore but headed upstairs.

He placed his gun in the kitchen drawer closest to him and closed it firmly. He was fully permitted to carry, but the last thing he needed was a hot headed cop freaking out at the sight of it.

He was already well into his explanation of what happened by the time Yara came back downstairs. The eyes of the older of the two patrolmen who'd been taking his statement grew comically big when Yara joined them.

In her usual blunt manner, she explained that they'd been in bed when they'd heard the sound of glass breaking and come down to find the shattered window and smoke-filled room.

To their credit, the officers had remained professional as she'd recited the facts, but Brandon didn't miss the looks they shot at each other. Although Yara hadn't been specific about what they'd been doing when the brick had come through the window, it was barely six in the morning and it was clear they'd been sharing a bed.

"I hope this doesn't cause you too much embarrassment," Brandon said after the patrolmen left with assurances that they'd be writing up a formal report that he could request for his insurance company after seventy-two hours.

Yara surprised him by taking three big steps forward and wrapping her arms around his waist. "I'm not embarrassed by my feelings for you."

He felt a goofy grin slide across his face despite the circumstances. "Do you have feelings for me?"

She rolled her eyes playfully. "As much as I have tried not to, I do have feelings for you."

He leaned forward, but she backed away.

"No. I still have to go to work, and it's even more important that I get cleaned up and present a professional facade."

His heart dropped. "You may not be embarrassed by your feelings, but the cops seeing you here with me is going to cause you problems, isn't it?"

She moved in close again, pressing her palm against his heart. "Don't worry, counselor. I can handle it. And more importantly, I think you're worth it."

Chapter Twenty

She wasn't delusional enough to believe that Lieutenant Wilson wouldn't have heard about patrol responding to the incident at Brandon's town house in the early morning hours and finding her there, having obviously spent the night in his bed. She had hoped that he'd at least show a modicum of discretion and keep whatever dressing-down he was primed to give to the four walls of his office. Apparently, that was too much to hope for.

She'd barely stepped into the bullpen when Lieutenant Wilson bellowed her name from his office. He stood in the door frame and made a show of slamming the door the moment she stepped through.

"I told you to close the Rutger case as a suicide," he yelled loud enough that there was no doubt the detectives on the other side of the door heard. He didn't bother to round the desk and sit. Better to stand, lording over her. Much more intimidating, or at least he probably thought so.

She'd dealt with enough cops and criminals who

thought they could intimidate her that it would take a lot more than crowding her personal space.

She adopted a parade-rest stance. "You said the home invasions took precedence. With our suspect in custody, I had the time to look more deeply into the Rutger case and I found a connection between Zachary Brooks and a friend of Tanya's." She quickly filled him in on what Bailey had told her and Brandon and Zachary Brooks's role as an informant and possible participant in the sale of illegal pills at the Stryder Medical Clinic.

"Just so I have this straight, you went behind my back to continue an investigation I ordered you to steer clear of?"

Of course that was all that the lieutenant would take from what she'd told him.

"With all due respect, sir, you did not order me to close the case. As such I treated it as I would any other suspicious death and investigated it until I was satisfied that it was a suicide, which for the record, I never believed."

Wilson scowled. "And your conclusion that this case is a homicide wouldn't have anything to do with the fact that you're sleeping with the victim's attorney?"

She couldn't help it, she flinched. Her fellow detectives had heard that. What were they thinking?

"Brandon West is neither a suspect nor a witness in this matter or any other case on my desk," she bit out. "As such, what we do on my personal time is of no concern—"

"I decide what is of concern in my unit, Detective. And it concerns me that I gave an order and you not only disregarded it, you conducted a rogue investigation with a civilian. Do you have anything to say for yourself?"

With ten years under her belt as a female law enforcement officer, she'd become an expert at forcing her anger into a tiny little box and locking it away. But this time it wouldn't be tangled. "You know what, I do have something to say. You're a crap lieutenant." She kept her voice low so her coworkers wouldn't hear, her only concession to the fact she was currently telling off her boss and likely diminishing her career prospects.

The lieutenant took a step back, shock written across his face.

"The evidence in this case screamed that this was no suicide right from the beginning, but you only care about clearing cases so that you look good to the higher-ups. So that nothing gets in the way of you climbing the bureaucratic ladder. Well, that's not why I became a cop. That's not why the detectives sitting out there bust their humps every day. Tanya Rutger deserves justice. Her family deserves to know why she died and who is responsible. And the community we serve deserves to know that we did everything we could to get a killer off the streets. So I did what I had to do. If there are consequences to be paid, so be it."

Her words, quiet though they were, had sucked

all the oxygen out of the room. They stood, silently assessing one another.

After a long moment, Wilson's eyes narrowed and his face twisted into an expression of fury. "Oh, there will be consequences. I'm writing you up and suggesting a lengthy suspension without pay. I wish I could do more but as of right now consider yourself on desk duty, indefinitely. You don't leave your desk for any reason without notifying me first. Do you understand?"

"Yes, sir," she said between gritted teeth.

"Now, get out of my office."

She opened the door, letting it bang against the sidewall. There was no use in trying to keep a low profile. Every eye in the bullpen was on her as she stalked across the floor to her desk and fell into her chair.

The low hum of voices picked up again as she logged on to her computer, careful to keep her gaze from landing on any of her coworkers. She didn't want to see the pity, or glee, in their eyes. She could already guess which of the other detectives were reveling in her downfall and those who felt sorry for her having demolished her career.

She'd done what she had to do to get justice, and despite everything, she knew she'd do it again. And she didn't think that made her a bad cop.

"Hey."

She looked up to see Martin leaning across his desk toward her.

"I wouldn't worry about the lieutenant too much. He's angry now but when this all washes out, he'll probably settle on a verbal reprimand and a note in your file."

Martin was probably right. Taking this any further would mean acknowledging to the brass that one of his detectives ran an investigation under his nose without his knowledge, and he was not going to spotlight his failure to supervise his squad like that. Too bad for her that didn't feel like much right now.

BRANDON'S PHONE BUZZED. He didn't recognize the number. "Hello."

"I finally got in."

He looked at the screen again but the number still wasn't registering. "Who is this?"

"Nick, Tanya's brother. I figured out Tanya's password for her cloud storage. I'm in and I listened to her video diary. I know who killed her." Nick's voice was a mixture of excitement and rage.

"Whoa, whoa, slow down and start from the beginning."

"I told you I was trying to figure out Tanya's cloud password since the police couldn't find her phone or tablet. I did. It was a combination of the address where we were living when she was born and our mom's current address. Anyway, I'm in and I started listening to her diary recordings. She was dating a doctor she worked with. He was the one paying for her apartment and Mercedes."

Brandon had a feeling he knew which doctor Tanya had been involved with, but he asked the question anyway. "Which doctor?"

"She called him Anand. That's the young one, right?"

"Yeah," Brandon answered, distractedly. The young married one.

"A few weeks ago she walked in on him selling pills to a patient. She confronted him about it and he threatened to cut off the money. She was going to go to the cops. That's why he killed her."

"Did she say that in the diary? That she was going to the cops and Anand threatened to kill her if she did?"

"She said she was going to the cops. She said he'd been good to her, paying for the apartment and car, so she wanted to give him a chance to tell his wife and get his affairs in order. She didn't…" Nick's words caught on a sob. "She didn't want to hurt him. That bastard. I'm going to kill him."

"Nick, you have got to calm down. Don't let your emotions lead you to do something you'll regret. You need to take Tanya's diary to the police. I'll go with you."

"The cops don't care," he screamed. "They think Tanya killed herself. I told them she would never, but they wouldn't listen."

"Nick, listen to me. Detective Thomas doesn't think Tanya committed suicide. She and I have been working together to prove it. If you take the diary to her, that will be enough to force her superiors to let her formally investigate Tanya's death as a murder."

"No. No, the cops had their chance." His voice was shrill. "I'm going to do what needs to be done now. That doctor's address is in Tanya's contacts. I've got my father's old gun. I'm going to go to his house and kill him and no one is going to stop me."

"Nick!"

The only answer was dead air. Nick had hung up on him.

Brandon pulled up the file Shawn had sent to him on Anand Gristedes and jotted down his address. He turned to the wall behind his desk and pressed a finger to the top left corner of the third panel of wainscoting lining the bottom. The panel popped free, revealing the safe behind it. He pressed his palm to the faceplate and seconds later the safe unlocked.

His Ruger lay in the safe already loaded. He might not have an official role in West Security and Investigations, but he was still a West. James West Sr. had made sure all his sons knew how to defend themselves. He was more than proficient with a gun.

He stuck the weapon in his waistband, then darted from his office. His paralegal was on the phone but he glanced up as he raced from the office.

He started his car and pulled into traffic before ordering the onboard system to dial Yara's cell phone.

She picked up after three rings. "Now's not a good time."

"Nick Rutger is on his way to Anand Gristedes's house. He got into Tanya's cloud file and listened to her video diary. Tanya apparently saw Gristedes selling pills to a patient and was planning to turn him in. Nick thinks Gristedes killed her to stop her. He's got a gun and he's saying he's going to kill Gristedes."

Yara swore. "Where are you?"

"I'm on my way to Gristedes's place, too."

"No, that is a bad idea. I want you to stay out of this."

"I think it's too late for that, Yara. I'm right in the middle of this and I'm not going to let Tanya's brother throw his life away."

"Damn it, Brandon. Listen to me. If Nick is right, Gristedes already killed one person. And I doubt he could have been selling pills out of the clinic without Dr. Manning and who knows who else knowing or being involved with what was going on. You have no idea what you're walking into."

"I get that, but it also means that Nick has no idea either. I can't let him do it alone."

"Brandon, Gristedes won't hesitate to kill you and Nick if that's what he thinks will get him out of the mess he's made. He has nothing to lose."

"I don't doubt it," he said, cutting off an SUV and drawing an angry car horn. "But I can't just sit back and hope that this young man cools off before he does something foolish. Hopefully, I'm able to get to Gristedes's place and stop Nick."

"And what if you don't get there in time?"

"That's why I'm calling you. For backup."

"I'm on my way, but Brandon, do not go inside Gristedes's house. Do not approach him. He could be dangerous. Try to get Nick to calm down and see reason if you can, but if you can't, don't follow him out of the frying pan into the fire. Do you understand me? I don't want to see you get hurt."

"It warms my heart to know you care."

"Brandon!"

"I'm two minutes away from Gristedes's place. Get a move on."

This time he disconnected the call.

He really did hope he was able to catch Nick before he got to Gristedes's, but if he didn't… He'd at least try to do for Tanya's brother what he hadn't been able to do for her.

He made it to Gristedes's house in record time. The home was in an upscale neighborhood with multi-acre properties that backed onto a protected forest area. The homes were spread far enough apart that there was no way a neighbor could hear or see much of anything happening on the adjacent properties. Which may have been terrific for privacy purposes, but it meant that no one was likely to see or hear any altercation taking place at the Gristedes home.

He was driving so fast that he passed the entrance for the driveway. He punched the brakes and threw the sports car into reverse before making the right turn.

The house was a large, white brick colonial with a traditional wide, wood-planked front porch surrounded by columns. A four-car garage jutted off one side of the house, but Brandon was more concerned by the black pickup truck that sat in front of the home.

Nick had beaten him here.

He stepped out of the car and made his way to the front door. He debated whether it made sense to ring the doorbell, alerting Gristedes to his presence, or attempt to make a more stealthy entrance. Before he could decide, raised voices came from inside.

"I know you killed my sister, admit it!" Nick's voice sounded close to losing control.

Brandon peeked through the window facing the porch. Nick and Gristedes stood in the living room.

Nick held Gristedes at gunpoint.

Gristedes's voice was too low for Brandon to make out his response, but whatever he'd said, it only made Nick angrier.

"Liar!" Nick screamed.

Brandon tried the front door and found it unlocked. He pulled his gun from his waistband, but held it down against his leg. Nick was distraught, but Brandon didn't believe he wanted to kill Gristedes. If he did, he'd have shot the man by now. He was a grieving brother and if Brandon wanted to make sure he did everything he could to talk him down off the ledge he'd climbed out on before resorting to extreme measures, he had to be careful.

He stepped into the house and approached the living room. "Nick."

Nick's gaze swung toward him, but his gun didn't waver. "What are you doing here?"

"Trying to stop you from making the biggest mistake of your life."

"He killed my sister."

"I know. And so does Detective Thomas. I called her and told her everything you told me. She believed me. She believes you. You don't need to do this."

Nick shook his head, tears streaming down his

face. "I do. Even if you and that detective believe me, he has money. He'll get good lawyers. They'll get him off. He has to pay for what he did to Tanya."

"And he will. He will, Nick. No lawyer in the world will be able to get him off of drug and murder charges. Tanya would not want you to throw your life away like this. Not for her."

Nick sobbed, but still managed to hold the gun steady.

"Why don't you give me the gun." Brandon moved forward cautiously. "We can call Detective Thomas and hold Gristedes until she gets here. Let's do this the right way, Nick."

Out of the side of his eye, Brandon saw Gristedes's expression darken, but he wisely kept quiet.

Nick hiccupped, then his eyes grew wide.

Brandon felt the person behind him a moment too late. He turned, catching sight of Dr. Manning before something crashed down on his head.

He staggered, falling to his knees. His gun skittered across the floor and under the sofa. It was difficult to hold on to consciousness. He could hear a struggle taking place behind him. His gaze swam, but he was able to make out Nick and Gristedes fighting for the gun. Dr. Manning stood over Brandon still holding the lamp he'd used to smash him over the head. But now he seemed paralyzed by the unusual scene before him, unable to decide what to do next.

Gristedes landed a punch to Nick's jaw that sent him reeling backward. Unfortunately, his gun flew forward, landing several feet away from Nick and far too close to Gristedes.

The younger doctor lunged for the weapon.

"Run!" Brandon yelled to Nick.

Nick took off through the opening that led to the kitchen.

Gristedes grabbed the gun from the floor, but when he rose, Nick had already disappeared through the back of the house.

"Stay with him." Gristedes shot the order at Dr. Manning as he raced to catch up with Nick.

Dr. Manning didn't show any sign of having heard him. He stood staring out as if in some sort of fugue state.

Would he stay that way long enough for him to retrieve his gun from under the sofa?

There wasn't time to attempt doing so.

A gunshot blasted from the back of the house.

Brandon pushed to his feet and ran toward the sound.

Chapter Twenty-One

A string of swears rolled through Yara's mind but she didn't stop to vocalize them. She dashed from the office, her eyes roaming the bullpen for Martin. Her eyes landed on him coming out of the kitchen with a pretty uniformed officer at this side.

"Martin. With me." The tone of her voice must have clued him in to the gravity of the situation. He thrust the cup he was holding into the hands of the officer and dashed toward her. He caught up with her as she hit the crash bar on the exit door.

They stepped outside into a crisp wind. Daytime traffic streamed by the police station, the commuters more concerned with their destinations than the two detectives dashing from the building.

"What's up?" Martin asked as they ran for her police-issued vehicle.

Yara unlocked the car and wrenched the driver's side door open. "Tanya Rutger's brother was able to access her video diary. She was having an affair with Dr. Anand Gristedes and caught him selling medication under the table. She was going to the authorities and Nick is convinced that Gristedes killed her to stop her. He's headed for Gristedes's place now."

"Have you alerted dispatch we'll need backup?"

She swore out loud this time. It looked like Nick and Brandon weren't the only ones letting emotion get the best of them. "No, do that now. And have them confirm Gristedes's address. I know he lives in one of those big houses on the block, but I want to confirm I've got the address correct."

Martin made the call while she sped through the streets of Silver Hill, the siren blaring. Gristedes's house wasn't far from the station, but traffic was heavy, adding time to the drive that she didn't have.

She finally turned onto Gristedes's narrow curved road. Martin had confirmed the address with dispatch and when they came to the house, they found the large wrought iron gates already open. She gunned the sedan up the inclined circular drive and stopped behind Brandon's black BMW. A black pickup truck was parked in front of it.

"That's Brandon's car there."

"And the tags on the truck match Nick's registration."

Yara opened the driver's side door. "Damn it, I told him not to go inside."

"That's advice we should take, too. Backup is two minutes out."

A gunshot came from inside the house.

Ice shot through her veins. "We can't wait. We have to go inside. Now."

They entered the house with their guns drawn.

Dr. Manning stood in the middle of the living room, clutching a broken lamp.

"Put the weapon down and get your hands on the back of your head," Yara barked.

Manning didn't move.

Martin yanked the lamp from his hand and pulled his arms behind his back. Manning put up no resistance. It was like his body was there, but he was lost somewhere in his own head.

"Go," Martin said, pulling his handcuffs from his belt. "I've got him."

Yara made her way through the house, clearing the dining room before heading to the kitchen. The back door stood open, and as she approached it, she could hear the sound of male voices.

"It's over, Gristedes. The police know what you did. There's no point in killing us," Brandon said.

Anand Gristedes held Brandon and Nick at gunpoint at the far end of the large yard. Nick lay on the ground, clutching his side as blood poured out through a gunshot wound. Brandon stood with his hands in the air several feet away. He didn't appear to be hurt, thank God.

"If the cops know what I did, I'm going to jail no matter what. I may as well end the people who put me there." He pointed the gun at Brandon.

Yara stepped out of the house, her gun aimed at Gristedes. "Drop it, Gristedes, or I will shoot you!"

Gristedes sent a wild-eyed, panicked look her way but kept his gun trained on Brandon. "I don't think so, Detective Thomas. You put your gun down now or I'll shoot him."

"You know that is not going to happen," Yara said, making her way toward the men.

"Stop where you are or I will shoot!" Gristedes screamed, the hand holding the gun shaking.

She stopped. "Think this through, Dr. Gristedes. You can leave here in handcuffs or a body bag, but those are your only choices right now. Think about your wife. Your kids. They wouldn't want you to do something you can't take back."

"My wife and kids," he said with derision. "My wife left me. She took the kids. She didn't believe me when I said I had nothing to do with Tanya's death."

Smart woman. Not smart enough to get rid of Gristedes earlier, but better late than never.

"If you pull that trigger you'll never have the chance to explain things to her. You'll never have the chance to patch things up."

"I can't fix this. You know that as well as I do. I killed Tanya. She found out about my side business. A few pills here and there. To people who wanted them! Needed them! I wasn't pushing coke to kids. These were adults. How did she think I was paying for that damn apartment of hers, huh? The Mercedes? She didn't have a problem accepting the money until she knew where it was coming from. Then she wanted to get on her high horse. She should have just minded her business."

No matter how he justified it, he'd just admitted to murder.

"Gristedes, think about what you're doing here," Brandon said in a low soothing voice.

"I have thought about it. You don't have any idea how much I've thought about it. I can't go to jail. I just can't go to jail."

Gristedes swung the gun toward her, but before she could get off a shot, Brandon launched himself at the man.

They went down with a hard thud but Gristedes didn't let go of his gun. She didn't have a clear shot and she wasn't going to take the chance she'd hit Brandon by mistake.

Brandon grabbed a hold of Gristedes's gun hand at the same time the man reared up, throwing Brandon to the side. In a testament to how determined he was, Brandon didn't let go of the man's hand. Brandon banged the gun against the ground once, twice, before Gristedes finally lost his grip. The gun fell to the side.

"Freeze!" she yelled, the command aimed at both men.

But they ignored her. With them still locked in battle, she didn't have a clear shot.

The doctor reared up again, head-butting Brandon. They rolled, Gristedes ending up on top. He threw a wild punch that landed on Brandon's neck. Brandon's aim was more accurate. His punch landed on Gristedes's temple. Gristedes fell to the side, dazed but only for a moment. He noticed the gun within arm's reach and scrambled for it.

Yara got there first. She kicked the gun away and

held her own on Gristedes. "I don't think so. On your stomach, hands behind your head."

Gristedes looked up at her. For a brief moment, she thought he just might try to rush her, but then Brandon was there, pushing the man onto his stomach.

The sound of sirens came from the front of the house. Martin burst through the back door, his gun drawn.

She handcuffed Gristedes while Martin kept his gun trained on the man in case he decided to make one last stand at getting away.

Officers flooded the backyard and someone yelled for EMTs to be called.

She made her way over to where Brandon crouched, now only in his undershirt, pressing his button-down shirt to the side of Nick's torso.

"Don't worry," he said to Nick. "The paramedics are on their way. You're going to be okay."

Yara watched the blood soaking Brandon's shirt and hoped he was right.

Chapter Twenty-Two

The hospital wasn't busy, thankfully, and both Brandon and Nick were taken back to be treated right away. Brandon was receiving treatment for the bump on his head and Nick had been whisked into surgery to remove the bullet in his stomach. Martin had gone back to the station to get Gristedes and Dr. Manning processed.

That left Yara sitting in the ER waiting room alone, anxious for word on Brandon's and Nick's conditions.

A little more than an hour after she arrived, Martin called to let her know that Manning was already yelling about making a deal. He'd agreed to rat out all the players in the scheme—Gristedes and several pharmacists who had been involved in one way or another in selling medications on the side. They'd been doing it for years apparently, but Gristedes had taken things up a notch in the last year, selling far more than the others thought was advisable. With a wife, two kids and a girlfriend with expensive tastes, he'd needed the extra cash. The prescriptions had caught the attention of the state medical board, which had contacted the state and federal authorities, kicking off the investigation into the Stryder Medical Clinic. The district attorney and the state medical board were working together now to permanently shut down the clinic.

Gristedes was still refusing to talk but Yara doubted they'd need his testimony. He'd all but confessed to Tanya's murder at the house while he was holding the gun on Brandon and Nick. He was going away for a very long time.

A pregnant woman waddled in, guided by her harried-looking husband. One of the nurses at the admittance desk jumped to attention right away, grabbing a wheelchair and guiding the woman into it. The daddy-to-be looked as if he might need a wheelchair of his own. Yara was pretty sure he wouldn't make it through the birth without passing out. With practiced ease, the nurse guided the couple through the registration process, then pushed the woman toward an elevator, her husband trailing behind.

A moment later, the doors to the ER swung open and Brandon emerged. She stood, drawing his attention to her, and they met in the center of the room.

"How are you?" She let her eyes trail over him. With the exception of a white bandage over his left eye, he didn't look any worse for wear.

"The doctor says I'm fine. No concussion. Just a little cut over my eye. Must have gotten it in the scuffle with Gristedes. A couple of stitches, a few aspirin—" he waved the small square pack in his hands at her "—and I'm as good as new. Any word on Nick's condition?"

"He's in surgery. The doctors can't tell me much because I'm not next of kin. His mother is here, up on the surgery floor with a friend from her church. It might be several hours before they know anything, though."

"I should go up and sit with her." Brandon turned toward the elevators, the sudden movement causing him to wince. He pressed two fingers to the bandage on his head.

She reached out to steady him. "You're hurt. You should go home and rest. Mrs. Rutger will understand. You can call her tomorrow."

"Maybe you're right," he conceded, only slightly begrudgingly.

"Come on. I'll take you home."

Brandon was silent during the drive.

Yara pulled into a space in front of his house. That he didn't balk at her helping him to the door, taking his key and unlocking it for him told her everything she needed to know about the pain he was in. She helped him to the master bedroom and into bed, then returned to the kitchen for a glass of water so he could take his pain medication.

Brandon's eyes remained closed as she reentered the bedroom and placed the water on the nightstand next to the bed. "I think I should stay with you tonight. Just to keep an eye on you. No funny business."

He opened his eyes and smiled, cheekily. "I don't know if I want you to stay if there's going to be no funny business."

She felt a small smile bloom. Even with a head wound, the man didn't fail to be charming. "You talk a good game, but you look like you're ready to fall down. There's no way you could even manage funny business tonight."

"With you, I think I'll always be up for a little funny business."

His eyes softened, and her chest filled with emotion. She could have lost him today. The idea hit her with a force she hadn't thought was possible.

"How about you take a hot shower and then get back into bed while I get you something to eat. If you're still awake after that, I'll put on a comedy. That's all the funny business you're going to get tonight."

All she wanted to do was curl up next to him and hold him. To keep him at her side and know he was safe.

"Hey." He caught her hand as she started to move toward the kitchen. "I'm okay, you know. I'm okay."

It was his eyes, the sincerity, the honesty there, that convinced her more than anything that he wasn't really hurt.

She reached up with her free hand and rested it against his cheek. A wave of emotion welled in her chest. "When I saw Gristedes holding that gun on you, I've never been so scared in my life."

"And when you burst through that door, ready to kill to protect me, I've never seen anything so beautiful in my life. Yara, I'm not sure how it happened, but somewhere during this investigation I fell in love with you."

Her heart galloped with the force of his words. "You did?"

"I did. And I'm just hoping you feel a fraction of what I feel. I know you weren't ready before, but I'm willing to wait as long as it takes. Maybe with time—"

"I love you, too."

His eyes went wide. "You do?"

She threw her arms around his neck and leaned in to kiss him, drawing back before their lips met when he winced. "Oh, sorry. Did I hurt you?"

He pulled her in tightly against his chest. "Don't be. It's absolutely worth a little pain to hear you say those words."

She laughed, her heart soaring with the knowledge that he loved her as much as she loved him. "I'll say them every day if you want. Just so long as you keep saying them back."

He bent his head until his lips met hers. "As you wish."

Chapter Twenty-Three

Yara reclined on a lounge chair on Brandon's back deck. They were sharing a glass of exquisite red wine, watching the sunset and just enjoying being in each other's company. Brandon had lit the firepit and they sat close enough for the heat to warm them and for the flames to throw shadows across Brandon's chiseled jaw. It had been a little more than a month since she'd brought Brandon home from the hospital, and they'd spent nearly every night together. He'd recovered from his head wound nicely, suffering only a few bouts of dizziness. The hardest part of the recovery had been getting him to sit down and rest.

She'd been surprised by just how quickly she'd fallen into being part of a couple. The quick texts or calls determining what to have for dinner and whose place they'd stay at that night. She'd even acquiesced to a barbecue at Brandon's house that had brought his brothers and their families together with Sasha, Eddie and Miss Hanny. Her older brother, Henry, had promised to make a trip home soon so he could meet Brandon.

She stole another look at Brandon, her heart fluttering.

Things were moving fast, but it felt…right.

As if he sensed her thoughts, Brandon turned his head and looked at her, smiling. "You hungry?"

She returned his smile. "Starving."

They still had a lot to learn about each other, but one thing they'd already established was that if they were to have home-cooked meals beyond spaghetti, it was he who would have to do the cooking.

He leaned over and pressed his lips against hers for a quick, sweet moment before rising. "I made a spinach-and-chicken casserole. Let me just pop it in the oven."

Her phone rang as she disappeared inside.

"Thomas."

"Gristedes wants to deal," Martin said, skipping a greeting.

"Manning is talking. We don't need to make a deal to lock up Gristedes."

Manning had started talking to Morgan from the moment of his arrest and hadn't stopped giving up the names of the people involved in the far-reaching prescription drug scam. He'd given the federal authorities details on how he'd gotten hooked up with the fake prescription drug ring years earlier. After joining the practice, Dr. Gristedes had quickly figured out what was going on and demanded to be let in on the fraud, too. But Manning swore he'd had nothing to do with Tanya's murder and had agreed to testify against his former colleague in exchange for a lenient jail sentence.

"Yes, but District Attorney Morgan wants them both tied up tight. A plea will do that and put Manning and Gristedes away for most of the rest of their lives. Gristedes has admitted to coaxing Tanya into taking a drive with him. He got her to drive to Route 30, where he killed her and tried to make it look like a suicide before walking back to the interstate and picking up his car where he'd left it off the closest exit. He told us we would find the gun at his parents' hunting cabin. I've already got a warrant in the works and a call in to the local sheriff's office."

They'd searched Gristedes's home and found Tanya's computer hidden in a closet. Gristedes admitted to destroying her phone and tossing it, so they'd likely never find that. He'd also cleared Zachary Brooks of any involvement in Tanya's murder, but accused Zach of attempting to blackmail him about the fraud. That was probably one of the reasons Morgan was so keen on a plea with Gristedes. Having a key witness at trial who'd tried to blackmail the defendant while seeking a favor from the prosecution wasn't likely to boost Zach's credibility with a jury.

"How much time is the prosecutor offering?"

"Fifteen years on the prescription fraud and thirty years on the murder before he gets a shot at parole. It's not a bad deal."

It might not be a bad deal, but it wasn't good

enough. But it was likely the best they'd get and nothing would bring Tanya back.

"What about Nick?" Yara asked.

Nick Rutger was going to survive his gunshot wound, but he had been charged with criminal possession of a weapon and Brandon had made it his mission to get the charges dropped or reduced.

"The prosecutor handling the case still has to talk to your boyfriend, but she's going to offer to knock the charges down to a misdemeanor. Public sentiment is not on her side and she knows it. Nick won't do time."

She let out a breath as Brandon returned to the patio with another bottle of wine.

"Oh, one more thing," Martin said. "We finally tracked down Jasper Reinholt. He really did have a family emergency. His father had a heart attack and Jasper's been in the hospital by his side day and night with his phone shut off. That's why he didn't return our calls initially. The flight records check out. He's in the clear."

"Thanks for letting me know, Martin."

"Work?" Brandon's brow rose.

She filled him in on what Martin had told her while he poured them each another glass of wine.

"I saw I had a couple of voice mails. I guess I know what they are about now."

"Do you need to go deal with them now?"

He set the bottle down on the table next to their glasses and settled himself on the lounge chair next to her, wrapping his arms around her waist.

"It can wait. I'm right where I need to be at the moment."

Warmth fluttered through her that wasn't caused by the fire. She snuggled in closer to Brandon and he held her tighter.

"You know what, counselor? I think I am, too."

* * * * *

Look for another title in K.D. Richards's
West Investigations series when
A Stalker's Prey *goes*
on sale next month!

#2193 COLD CASE IDENTITY
Hudson Sibling Solutions • by Nicole Helm

Palmer Hudson has a history of investigating cold case crimes. Helping his little sister's best friend, Louisa O'Brien, uncover the truth about her biological parents should be simple. But soon their investigation becomes a dangerous mystery...complicated by an attraction neither can deny.

#2194 MONSTER IN THE MARSH
The Swamp Slayings • by Carla Cassidy

When businessman Jackson Fortier meets Josie Cadieux, a woman who now lives deep in the swamp, he agrees to help find the mysterious man who assaulted her a year earlier. Soon, Josie's entry into polite upper-crust society to expose the culprit changes Jackson's role from investigator to protector.

#2195 K-9 SECURITY
New Mexico Guard Dogs • by Nichole Severn

Rescuing lone survivor Elena Navarro from a deadly cartel attack sends Cash Meyers's bodyguard instincts into overdrive. The former marine—and his trusty K-9 partner—will be damned if she falls prey a second time...even if he loses his heart keeping her safe.

#2196 HELICOPTER RESCUE
Big Sky Search and Rescue • by Danica Winters

After a series of strange disappearances, jaded helicopter pilot Casper Keller joins forces with Kristin Lauren, a mysterious woman involved in his father's death. But fighting the elements, sabotage and a mission gone astray may pale in comparison to the feelings their reluctant partnership exposes...

#2197 A STALKER'S PREY
West Investigations • by K.D. Richards

Actress Bria Baker is being stalked. And her ex, professional bodyguard Xavier Nichols, is her best hope for finishing her movie safely. With Bria's star burning as hot as her chemistry with Xavier, her stalker is convinced it's time for Bria to be his...

#2198 THE SHERIFF'S TO PROTECT
by Janice Kay Johnson

Savannah Baird has been raising her niece since her troubled brother's disappearance. But when his dead body is discovered—and unknown entities start making threats—hiding out at officer Logan Quade's isolated ranch is their only chance at survival...and her brother's only chance at justice.

HICNM1223

Get 3 FREE REWARDS!

We'll send you 2 FREE Books plus a FREE Mystery Gift.

ONE NIGHT STANDOFF
NICOLE HELM

CANADA COUNTY
K-9 DETECTIVES
RACHEL LEE

HOTSHOT HERO IN DISGUISE

CAVANAUGH JUSTICE:
DETECTING A KILLER

FREE
Value Over
$20

Both the **Harlequin Intrigue®** and **Harlequin® Romantic Suspense** series feature compelling novels filled with heart-racing action-packed romance that will keep you on the edge of your seat.

YES! Please send me 2 FREE novels from the Harlequin Intrigue or Harlequin Romantic Suspense series and my FREE gift (gift is worth about $10 retail). After receiving them, if I don't wish to receive any more books, I can return the shipping statement marked "cancel." If I don't cancel, I will receive 6 brand-new Harlequin Intrigue Larger-Print books every month and be billed just $6.49 each in the U.S. or $6.99 each in Canada, a savings of at least 13% off the cover price, or 4 brand-new Harlequin Romantic Suspense books every month and be billed just $5.49 each in the U.S. or $6.24 each in Canada, a savings of at least 12% off the cover price. It's quite a bargain! Shipping and handling is just 50¢ per book in the U.S. and $1.25 per book in Canada.* I understand that accepting the 2 free books and gift places me under no obligation to buy anything. I can always return a shipment and cancel at any time by calling the number below. The free books and gift are mine to keep no matter what I decide.

Choose one: ☐ **Harlequin Intrigue Larger-Print** (199/399 BPA GRMX)   ☐ **Harlequin Romantic Suspense** (240/340 BPA GRMX)   ☐ **Or Try Both!** (199/399 & 240/340 BPA GRQD)

Name (please print)

Address   Apt. #

City   State/Province   Zip/Postal Code

Email: Please check this box ☐ if you would like to receive newsletters and promotional emails from Harlequin Enterprises ULC and its affiliates. You can unsubscribe anytime.

Mail to the Harlequin Reader Service:

IN U.S.A.: P.O. Box 1341, Buffalo, NY 14240-8531
IN CANADA: P.O. Box 603, Fort Erie, Ontario L2A 5X3

Want to try 2 free books from another series? Call 1-800-873-8635 or visit www.ReaderService.com.

*Terms and prices subject to change without notice. Prices do not include sales taxes, which will be charged (if applicable) based on your state or country of residence. Canadian residents will be charged applicable taxes. Offer not valid in Quebec. This offer is limited to one order per household. Books received may not be as shown. Not valid for current subscribers to the Harlequin Intrigue or Harlequin Romantic Suspense series. All orders subject to approval. Credit or debit balances in a customer's account(s) may be offset by any other outstanding balance owed by or to the customer. Please allow 4 to 6 weeks for delivery. Offer available while quantities last.

Your Privacy—Your information is being collected by Harlequin Enterprises ULC, operating as Harlequin Reader Service. For a complete summary of the information we collect, how we use this information and to whom it is disclosed, please visit our privacy notice located at corporate.harlequin.com/privacy-notice. From time to time we may also exchange your personal information with reputable third parties. If you wish to opt out of this sharing of your personal information, please visit readerservice.com/consumerschoice or call 1-800-873-8635. **Notice to California Residents**—Under California law, you have specific rights to control and access your data. For more information on these rights and how to exercise them, visit corporate.harlequin.com/california-privacy.

HIHRS23